ATTY AT LAW

ATTY AT LAW

TIM LOCKETTE

ILLUSTRATIONS BY DAVID WARDLE

TRIANGLE
SQUARE
books for young readers

NEW YORK • OAKLAND • LIVERPOOL

SEVEN STORIES PRESS
140 Watts Street
New York, NY 10013
www.sevenstories.com

College professors and high school and middle school teachers
may order free examination copies of Seven Stories Press titles.
To order, visit www.sevenstories.com/textbook
or send a fax on school letterhead to (212) 226-1411.

Library of Congress Cataloging-in-Publication Data

Names: Lockette, Tim, author. | Wardle, David (Illustrator), illustrator.
Title: Atty at law / Tim Lockette ; illustrations by David Wardle.
Description: New York : Triangle Square Books for Young Readers/
Seven Stories Press, [2020] | Audience: Grades 4-6. | Summary: Atticus "Atty"
Peale fights for the rights of animals, copes with having a racially-mixed family in small-town
Alabama, navigates the social scene of middle school, and determines to help
her father prove Jethro Gersham innocent of murder.
Identifiers: LCCN 2020009068 (print) | LCCN 2020009069 (ebook) |
ISBN 9781644210123 (hardcover) | ISBN 9781644210130 (ebook)
Subjects: CYAC: Criminal investigation--Fiction. | Middle schools--Fiction. |
Schools--Fiction. | Racially mixed people--Fiction. | Family life--Alabama--
Fiction. | Alabama--Fiction.
Classification: LCC PZ7.1.L6233 Att 2020 (print) |
LCC PZ7.1.L6233 (ebook) | DDC [Fic]--dc23
LC record available at https://lccn.loc.gov/2020009068
LC ebook record available at https://lccn.loc.gov/2020009069

Book design by Jon Gilbert

Printed in the USA.

9 8 7 6 5 4 3 2

For Dottie

1

Hanging out at the Strudwick County Animal Shelter is like holding a baby with a dirty diaper. It's the cutest thing in the world, if you can just stand the smell.

Imagine the cutest puppies you've ever seen. Labrador retrievers as brown as buttery biscuits. Baby beagles who wag their tails when you call them Snoopy. Now imagine every cat you've ever seen on the Internet. Clumsy yellow kittens with hair that sticks straight out, so their faces look like cartoon suns. Fat old gray kitties who look at you scornfully, like angry librarians.

Now imagine each of them in a cage made of chain-link fence. And imagine two rows of them down a long hallway. In a big cinder-block room with loud fans that blow the hot, humid air through. And the smell, everywhere, of a litter box that needs changing. A stink like the stink of the school bathroom. Even when it's cleaned up, the clean smell just reminds you of how stinky it was.

"I am not even here," Martinez said, not bothering to look up from his vintage Game Boy.

"Come on, man," I said. "Look how cute these puppies are! You've got to take a look."

"I'm about to level up," Martinez said. "Just find me a place to sit and do this. A place where nobody is barking."

Other girls have brothers who put their sisters in head-locks, or attack them with real darts, or mutilate their stuffed animals or show off their chewed-up food. I have Martinez, who wouldn't put me in a headlock unless I were a Pokémon or an orc. Real life is boring to Martinez. Every moment not spent in a fantasy world is a moment wasted.

"I bet I can find a dog so adorable, you'll have to put the game down," I told Martinez.

"Try me," he said, still not looking up.

It's this way all summer, every summer. Taleesa, my stepmom, is a freelance writer and photographer. In the summer, she drives all over Alabama, shooting photos and interviewing people, and she drags us along. We've been to the Burkeville Okra Festival, the Honda plant in Lincoln, the dragon boat races in Gadsden. We even waited for hours in the foyer of Holman Prison while Taleesa interviewed a guy on death row. I always bring a book, though usually I'm watching and listening. Martinez keeps his head down. When I close my eyes and think of him, I see him lit up in the blue light of a video game screen.

This time we were close to home, wandering around the Strudwick County Animal Shelter while Taleesa talked to the director about the stray animal problem.

So here we were in this cute, stinky place. I walked down

the row, searching for an animal to melt my brother's heart. In one cage, a basset hound waddled up and looked at me expectantly, as if I'd held out a treat. In another, a brown-and-white beagle writhed on the floor, trying to scratch his own back. I called him over for some through-the-fence scratching, but I guess I wasn't good enough at it, because he went back to his own spot.

"They're adorable, if you'd just look," I said.

"Mmmph," Martinez replied. "I'm fighting a boss."

Then I saw him. A mutt built like a Labrador, mostly black but with patches that were spotted black-and-white like a dalmatian. One eye completely circled by a black dot. Seeing me, the dog stood up, and for just a second he looked like one of those broad-chested bird dogs you see in the hunting magazines at Red Creek Barber Shop. But when he moved toward me, tail wagging, he seemed to crumple a little. He walked with a limp.

"Look at you," I said. The dog's nose was cold and his tongue warm as they pressed against my palm through the fence. "Look at you, you're hurt. Martinez, look, he's hurt!"

The dog had a big red welt down his left side.

"Ooh," Martinez said, finally pulled away from the game. "A bullet wound."

"Come on," I said. "Who'd shoot a dog like this? You're too obsessed with shooting things."

"How else would you get a big long gash like that? Grazed by a bullet, I'd say."

I didn't really want to think about what other ways a dog could get a big slash in his side. Sometimes I think that for boys like Martinez, shoot-'em-up stories are a kind of security blanket. As if a villain with a gun were the only thing that could hurt you.

"Want to take him out to play?" asked a voice behind us. It was Megg Sample, the woman who runs the animal shelter. Make that Miz Megg. She looked kind of official—like a Boy Scout troop leader—with her tan animal shelter uniform shirt and her short brown hair. She'd been sweet and friendly to us all morning, and yet somehow I got the feeling we should call her "ma'am." She had a no-nonsense air about her like a teacher who knows when you're lying.

"Can we take him out, Miz Megg? Really?" asked Martinez. Now the video game was snapped shut, and my little brother was a real, live nine-year-old.

"Absolutely," Megg said, opening the cage door and getting out the leash. The dog burst out of the cage to a kneeling Martinez, knocking him over and licking his face. "Now, now," Megg said. "Calm down. We'll get that energy out of you. Maybe it was a mistake to call you Easy."

"So that's his name," I said. "Easy."

"When he came to us yesterday, he had a collar," Megg said. "On the collar, a tag with the letter 'E.' No name of owner, no address. But he did have an immunization tag, so we know he's had his shots. Anyway, Easy seemed to fit. Just look at him. You're easy to get along with, aren't you, boy? Yes, you are."

I know. It's dumb to ask a dog questions, and then answer them yourself. But everybody does it, even me. Even Martinez, who would rather text than say the simplest things out loud.

After I got Easy on the leash, Megg led us out into the fenced-in courtyard beside the animal shelter. Slobbery rubber balls lay here and there on the grass.

"This is our play area," Megg said. "Easy's been limping a little, but he needs his daily workout. I'll leave you to it."

I've never seen Martinez happier. Easy did seem to favor the leg closest to the wound, but when Martinez threw the ball, he trotted to it, ears bouncing. Then he would bring the ball back and lay it at our feet, tail wagging, and look up with friendly brown eyes, as if we'd known him for years.

"I want a dog now," Martinez said. "I want this dog. He's magical."

I guess Martinez looked at me as he said it, but I was looking away. I'd heard the sound of a car door closing. Looking up, I saw a man walking across the parking lot, a man with a cloud of white hair, a flat face with beady brown eyes and eyebrows so faint it was like they didn't exist. Like Easy, he walked with a limp.

What caught my eye was the way he scowled at us. A long stare that seemed more than a little angry.

We get that sometimes. I'm white and my brother is black. It's not that hard to explain, really. My mom was white. A few years after she died, my dad married Taleesa. To me, the only odd thing about our family is that there are a couple of family members no one ever sees. Sometimes I feel like if we all sat down for an old-timey black-and-white picture, my mom would appear as a faint image behind Dad, like in a ghost story. Maybe I think of it that way because of what Taleesa always says about her first husband. He's "not in the picture."

So, we're like a lot of families. But other people don't always see it that way. They take long looks when we're out as a group, as if they're trying to figure out what we really are, or who goes with who. It's not all bad. When we went to Disney World, the cast members were always extra chipper when they saw us together, as if they were saying "Welcome to our country!" You'd think all that attention would get old, but I liked it.

Sometimes the whole thing is just funny. I remember one time we were at Walmart, and I was really annoyed with Martinez. Among other things, he wouldn't stop shaking boxes of Cheez-Its like they were maracas. I ordered him to stop, and I guess I was mean about it, because an old black woman shook her finger at me.

"Young lady," she said. "What gives you the right to talk to other people like that? This young man is not your servant to boss around. I don't care who you are or where you're from."

"Ma'am," I said. "He's my brother."

That changed everything. She turned on Martinez and cranked the anger up a notch. "You listen to your sister! Put those boxes down, stop being a fool! Your sister loves you, she's your elder, you need to have respect!" And on and on. It was awesome.

Anyway, this guy, limping across the parking lot, was not awesome. He glared at us. I glared right back. What else are you going to do with people like that?

Then Easy dropped the ball at my feet. My turn to play.

As I threw the ball, Martinez and I talked about whether or not we could convince Dad and Taleesa to let us have a dog. This dog.

"We'd have to do all the feeding and stuff," I warned. "Dad's in court all the time. Taleesa can barely remember to put her pants on in the morning, when she's writing."

Just then the door opened, and the cloudy-haired man limped out in to the courtyard, with Megg right behind him. He pointed at Easy.

"That's him," Cloudy Hair said. "That's the one that bit me. You need to put him down immediately."

Easy crouched at my feet, his tail wagging, his paws on either side of the slobbery red ball. That expectant, hey-there-friend look.

"Kids, step away from Easy," Megg said. "We may have a biting dog on our hands. I can't let you be near him."

Megg took the leash from me and reattached it to Easy's collar. When she leaned over to do it, Easy rolled over on his back, as if hoping for a tummy scratch.

"He doesn't look like a biting dog to me," Martinez observed.

"You want to see, boy?" Cloudy Hair said. "You want to see what he did to me?"

The man rolled up his pants leg and, sure enough, there was set of teeth marks on his right leg, all purple and black.

Megg hustled Easy back into the shelter and slammed him into his cage. Then she wrote a note and affixed it to the door. "SUSPECTED BITING DOG. NO RELEASE."

"This dog should be destroyed," Cloudy Hair said. "Under Alabama law a biting dog has to be destroyed."

I shuddered. Who talks like that? Who threatens to destroy someone? Just villains in the video games Martinez plays. Or so I thought.

"Not so fast," Megg said. "The law says a dog with no owner, if it bites someone, will be destroyed *after* the health officer does an investigation to determine that the dog has no owner."

Cloudy Hair's face scrunched up in a scowl for just a moment. Then: "Well, I'm the owner of the dog, then."

Megg crossed her arms. "Really? Prove it."

"What?" Cloudy Hair said, his voice cracking. "What are you talking about? Any fool can show up here and take a dog home. If I show up and say this is my dog, who's to say it isn't?"

"In my experience," Megg said. "People don't show up asking for their own dog to be put down. Come with me to the office, and we'll fill out some paperwork."

Now Cloudy Hair's face was flushed with rage. "This dog is *my property*," he said. "Why should I have to prove—"

"Hey, Mister," Martinez burst out, interrupting Cloudy Hair mid-sentence. "Hey! Hey! If this dog is yours, maybe you can explain why he has a bullet wound."

"I—I tried to shoot him after he bit me," Cloudy Hair said. "I missed him, and I been looking for him ever since."

"Are you going to shoot him now?" Martinez asked. "Is that why you got a gun?"

My brother pointed to Cloudy Hair's hip. Sure enough, under the tail of his flannel shirt, you could see a bulge of something attached to his belt just above his right butt cheek. Too small for a fanny pack, too big for a cell phone.

Maybe it was just instinct, but Cloudy Hair reached back and put his hand on whatever it was on his belt back there. Megg stepped between us and the old man, her hands up in front of her.

"That's it," she said. "Kids, you go out in the yard. Sir, if you do have a gun on your belt, I'm going to have to ask you to leave. That's not permitted here."

"I have a right to open carry under Alabama law," Cloudy Hair said.

"Not here you don't," Megg said.

Cloudy Hair stared Megg down for a second. Then he barked out a cussword and stormed out of the room, hitting the swinging door so hard it slapped against the wall.

Martinez and I didn't go out to the yard. Megg followed Cloudy Hair out of the room, and we followed her. Cloudy Hair stomped past the front desk and out the door to the parking lot, nearly plowing into a teenage volunteer who was cuddling a kitten. Megg went to the front desk and picked up the phone, holding the receiver as she watched Cloudy Hair climb into his truck and squeal out of the parking lot.

"You were about to call 911," I said.

Megg nodded.

"Sheriff's office," she said. "We work with them a lot. They know us."

"Well, I'm glad he's gone," Martinez said. "Can we go back and play with Easy, Miz Megg?"

Megg shook her head vigorously. "Oh, no," she said. "If we've got a report of a dog bite, even from somebody we don't like, we consider that dog a biting dog." She sighed. "So Easy will get the treatment any other dangerous dog would get."

That made me feel queasy.

"Destroyed," I whispered. "That's what he said. That's what's going to happen to Easy."

What a word, "destroyed." I imagined a dog being locked into some mad scientist's machine and blasted into millions of green atoms.

Megg nodded.

"If someone else doesn't show up to claim the dog, we'll put him down," she said. "A little injection, and he falls asleep painlessly. And never wakes up."

Martinez, who'd killed a thousand dragons on a Nintendo screen, looked like he'd seen a zombie.

"How can you do that?" he asked. "To a doggie? Just kill it."

"It's terrible," Megg said, "But it's something we have to do. There's not enough room here for all the stray animals in Strudwick County, and not enough people adopting them. So every third Monday of the month, we put down two dozen or so. It's heartbreaking to do it to any of them. But I couldn't put down an innocent dog to make room for one suspected of biting."

"But Easy is innocent," I said. "Innocent until proven guilty. What if that man shot first, and then Easy bit him in self-defense? It's not fair."

"It's *not* fair," Megg agreed. "But under the law, animals are property. They don't speak for themselves. Owners speak for them. And unless an owner shows up by the next time we put animals down, Easy will be on the list."

"And when is that?" I asked.

"This coming Monday," Megg said. "Three days from now."

My heart sank.

2

'm weird about crying. I've never shed a tear over my own mother's death. I never knew her, really. But when Taleesa's dad died, I lost it.

I'd never met the man. I never saw him before I walked up to the casket. I was shivering. We'd flown up to Milwaukee in a hurry, and our Alabama winter clothes weren't warm enough for the cold. Every woman in the church was wearing a hat, the way they do in some black churches, and Taleesa and I didn't have hats. The whole family walked down the aisle and looked into this casket where a bald, dignified-looking man looked like he was sleeping with his hands folded. His suit was salmon-colored. I remember a tiepin with a big rhinestone on it.

"This is your namesake," Taleesa whispered to my brother. "You're named after him, Martinez."

I looked at the stranger in the casket. Martinez. And then I came totally unglued. Crying out loud. Shoulders shaking, snot running. As Dad pulled me away, everybody stared at the white girl with no coat or hat who'd suddenly gone crazy. To this day, when I hear the word "Milwaukee," I just want to crawl under the table.

I cried like that on the way home from the animal shelter. In the back seat, Martinez sat staring blankly, with no video game screen in front of him for once. That's his version of crying. Taleesa said nothing. That's one reason I like Taleesa better than most grown-ups. She never tells you it's going to be okay when it's not going to be okay.

"They say that dogs can experience grief, just like humans do, when they lose their owners," Taleesa said. "I bet there are some dogs at the shelter that are just as sad as you are now."

"But why do they have to kill them?" I said. "I mean, I know they can't afford to feed them all. But they don't get a trial or anything. They don't get to defend themselves. Miz Megg is supposed to be their friend, and she injects poison into them and lets them die."

"Believe me, Miz Megg *is* their friend," Taleesa said. "Why else would she work in that smelly place, cleaning up all that poop?"

"I know," I said. "I know. It's just—it's the fact that we *know* it's going to happen, and we can't stop it. All on the word of one man who wouldn't even give his name. Without a trial."

"Now you sound like your dad," Taleesa said.

I guess I should have mentioned that my dad is a lawyer. Sometimes I feel like he's *the* lawyer in Houmahatchee, Alabama. He does what they call "indigent defense," which means that if someone gets arrested and they're too poor to hire a lawyer, the State of Alabama hires my dad to defend them in court.

It's not what it looks like on TV. On TV, when people get arrested, the cops say "If you can't afford a lawyer, one will be provided for you," which sounds like you'll get a lawyer for free. In real life, the state pays my dad, and then it turns around and charges his clients for part of the cost. On TV, there's always a trial, with a lawyer pacing around the witness stand, asking tough questions. In real life, lawyers sit in a room and make a deal, and most people plead guilty to something, something a little less scary than what they were charged with.

Dad hates that part of the job. And he loves being in court, even if it's just to present a guilty plea. Which is why, when we got home, we were surprised to see his car in the driveway. When we came in, we found him in the den, still wearing his suit, ironing shirts and watching *Reversal of Fortune*, an old movie he's seen a thousand times.

"City prosecutor's got the flu," he said. "They postponed everything."

"Great," Taleesa said, kissing him on the cheek. "You can keep the kids while I go write my story."

"All right," Dad said, glancing up at me. "So, why has everybody been crying? Both of you. I can tell."

So, while Dad ironed and Taleesa typed on her laptop in the kitchen, I told Dad everything. When I was done, he just nodded.

"Interesting case," he said.

"It's not fair," I said. "We should change the law. There ought to be some way for a dog to get a fair chance."

"Well, now, wait a minute," Dad said. "What does the law actually say? People can talk all they want about what the law says. It's what's in the law books that matters."

"You mean Easy might have a chance?" Martinez and I glanced at each other with a smile.

"I mean, let's read the law," Dad said. "I've got a copy of the Criminal Code on the bookshelf in the dining room."

Yes, we have law books in the dining room. There's hardly a wall in our house that isn't covered with bookshelves, plus stacks of books on chairs and in corners. We've never needed the Dewey decimal system. The law books are all Dad's, anything with a dragon or wizard on the cover is mine, and Martinez owns all the weird manga with guys whose hair looks like a flame. Everything else—a thousand books on everything from fish-farming to the British royal family—is Taleesa's.

Martinez found it first. *The Criminal Code of Alabama 1975*, a book in fake black leather, fat as a Bible. He riffled through it.

"Bleah, a big long index," he said. "I hate looking in the index. That's what computers are for. *You* look it up."

```
Dog bite. See Animal Law.
```

Under Animal Law,

```
anacondas, bear-baiting,
```

cattle this and cattle that, cruelty . . . there,

```
dog bites.
```

That led us to another book, an even bigger one. *Code of Alabama Section 3—Animals.* Here's what it said:

> 3-6-1. If any dog shall, without
> provocation, bite or injure any person
> who is at the time and place where he
> has the legal right to be, the owner of
> the dog shall be liable in damages to
> the person bitten or injured . . .

And after that, a bunch of stuff about how you can know when a person is legally on the property of another person, and all the different ways an owner can argue he doesn't have to pay for a dog bite.

"Dad, this isn't about dogs," I said. "This is all about dog owners."

"Is there a section on rabies?" Dad asked.

> Whenever the rabies officer or the
> health officer shall receive information
> that a human being has been bitten or
> exposed by a dog or cat required to be
> immunized against rabies, the health
> officer or his authorized agent shall
> cause said dog or cat to be placed
> in quarantine. . . . When said dog
> or cat is unowned, as determined by
> the health officer after a reasonable
> investigation, or where the owner of
> the dog or cat agrees in writing, the

```
animal shall be immediately destroyed
and the head shall be submitted for
rabies examination to the state health
department.
```

I gasped. Martinez tried to look over my shoulder and see what was the matter, but I snatched the book away from him. *The head.* No need for him to see that.

Dad looked the book over. "You might have a case here."

"I don't see how," I said. "Easy has no owner. And the only person claiming to be the owner is the guy who wants him put down."

"Read it again," Dad said. "With a pen and paper. Read the whole section, and write down every phrase you think can help you."

Martinez and I sat at the dinner table and made a list.

"Required to be immunized against rabies," Martinez said. "But every dog's required to be immunized. So what does that mean?"

"I think it means a dog that isn't *already* immunized," I said. "And we know Easy has had his shots. So we write that down. And look at this: There's supposed to be a 'reasonable investigation' to find the owner of the dog. Has that happened? I don't think so."

"Well," Martinez said. "Cloudy Hair did say he was the owner, and Megg asked him for proof. Is that a reasonable investigation? What does 'reasonable investigation' mean? Heck, what does 'owner' mean, really?"

"Look at the beginning of the chapter," Dad shouted from the laundry room. "Every law starts with a definition of terms."

I looked and looked, but couldn't find any definitions at all. Dad looked over my shoulder as he passed through the dining room.

"To be honest," he said, "'reasonable' could mean anything. And 'owner' comes up so much in law, maybe they didn't define it."

"But owning an animal isn't like owning a car or a chair," I said. "At lot of this stuff says 'anyone who owns or keeps.' So if you feed a stray, and keep him as a pet, and then he bites somebody, you're responsible, even though you haven't bought the dog."

Dad nodded. "All very good points. Keep thinking."

I sat and read for a long time. Martinez wandered off to play a game. In the living room, Dad's movie ended, and in the quiet, I could hear Taleesa typing her story. Bangs and clatters from the kitchen as Dad tried to figure out what to cook for dinner. When I looked up from the book, the tree-shadows on the dining room curtains let me know it was late in the afternoon.

And then I had it. I rushed into the kitchen, where Dad was putting a frozen pizza in the oven.

"Dad," I said. "A dog can't commit a crime. Under the law, a dog isn't a person, he's property."

"True," Dad said.

"So it's all about ownership. The owner of a biting dog has to pay damages if that dog bites somebody. Only a dog with rabies has to be killed. Or a dog that *might* have rabies, because he hasn't had his shots, or because nobody knows whether he's had shots or not."

"I suppose that's true," Dad said. "You read the law."

"So they . . . they put dogs to sleep at the shelter every month because they don't have room for them. But the law says they have to keep them for a certain time so the owner can claim them, if they have an owner."

"Go on."

"So Easy isn't rabid. Cloudy Hair could be an owner. And if he is, he could also be a dog abuser. We don't know whether he shot first, or Easy bit first."

"All very true."

"But what if he's just a guy who hates his neighbor's dog? What if he goes onto someone else's property to kill his neighbor's barking dog? And he misses. And the dog bites him?"

"Plausible, I suppose," Dad said.

"So the owner should have a reasonable amount of time to claim Easy, right?" I said. "If Cloudy Hair is the owner, let him come back and prove it. And if there's another owner, give him a chance to come forward."

"Makes sense to me."

"Dad," I said. "You've got to take this to court. You've got to save that dog."

"Why me?" Dad asked. "Why not you?"

"I'm just a kid."

"So? You can write in English, can't you? Write up a brief and submit it to the court on Monday. You don't have to be a lawyer. Anybody can represent themselves in court. All you have to do is come up with a way that you, personally, have a stake in the case."

"What do you mean by a stake?" I asked.

"A dog can't make a claim before the court," Dad said. "It

has to be a human, and it has to be a human who's involved in the case in some way."

"But I don't have a stake," I said. "I'm not the owner."

"You know, there was a case years ago where an environmental group sued to stop the U.S. government from helping build a dam in Egypt," Dad said. "The dam was going to hurt, I don't know, a native fish or something. And the courts ruled against the environmentalists, because they didn't have a stake. But they said that if one member of the group had just bought a plane ticket to go look at the river as a tourist, they would have had a claim."

I thought for a minute.

"If *we* wanted to adopt Easy, then we'd have a reason to go to court, right?" I asked. "Dad, can we get a dog?"

From the bedroom, I heard a muffled "Noooo!" Then Taleesa came out.

"No dog," she said. "Not that one, anyway."

"But Easy's a sweet dog," I said. "And he'll die if we don't."

Taleesa sighed.

"I guess I'll be the grown-up here, since Paul won't," she said. "As a parent, I have to take care of my babies. You think I'm going to let a dog in here that's been accused of biting its owner? It's one thing to stand up for the accused, Paul. It's another thing to bring them into your house."

"I've already played with Easy," I said. "He's not going to hurt anybody."

"Hold on, hold on," Dad said. "Maybe we don't have to adopt Easy to take this case to court. Maybe there's another way."

Martinez marched back into the room, video game in

hand. "You're doing this all wrong, Atty. This is no way to get a dog. You're supposed to do it like I did with my fish. First, you wait till everything's sweet and cozy and happy, and then you look up at Mom and say, 'Gee, can I get a fish?' Then you draw pictures of goldfish and put them up on the fridge. Then you start watching *Finding Nemo* all the time and saying a fish would make you really happy. You've got to work on parents for a long time if you want to get a pet."

Eureka! Martinez cringed a little as I gave him a big hug.

"That's it! That's it!" I said. "That's the answer."

Everybody looked at me like I was crazy.

"It's simple," I said. "If Martinez and I were grown-ups, one of us would have adopted Easy already. Because, as grown-ups, we'd have the ability to do that. But we're kids. If we want to adopt a pet, we have to convince our parents. And that takes time. Taleesa, did the animal shelter people tell you how long they normally keep a dog before they put it to sleep?"

"At least three weeks," Taleesa said. "On the third Monday of every month, they put down every animal that's been there for at least three weeks without being adopted."

"So if he weren't a biting dog—and he isn't—he wouldn't be put down this coming Monday, because he's only been in the shelter for a day or so," I said. "So Martinez and I would have a month to convince you, our parents, to let us adopt him. By killing Easy on Monday, they're denying me and Martinez our right to own Easy the only way we can. It's doesn't matter if you want to adopt him today, Taleesa. What matters is that you *might* change your mind within a month."

Dad beamed.

"My lands," he said. "That might just work. That's . . . gosh, that's kind of brilliant."

"So what do I do next?" I asked. "How do I take that to court?"

"Well, you'd have to write a legal brief," Dad said. "Basically, it's a statement you give to the court to explain what you're asking for. Then you'd have to go before a judge and argue your case. I won't lie to you, both things are hard. The writing is hard, and getting up in front of a judge is hard. And with any case, there's a good chance you'll lose. Are you sure you want to do this?"

I thought of Easy's ears flopping as he ran after a slobbery ball.

"Time's wasting, Dad," I said. "Show me how to get started."

3

We can talk later about how courts and judges go all the way back to the Middle Ages, and how all the strange customs of the court—I mean, who wears robes in public, really?—started hundreds of years ago. For now, just know that when you ask a judge for something, you have to write it in very formal, old-timey language that's even worse than those five-paragraph essays you have to write in school. Dad tried to explain it all to me, but I hate being told how to write. So he left me with a stack of old legal briefs and his laptop, and told me to figure it out myself.

```
Comes now Atticus Tutwiler Peale,
acting on her own behalf, and moves
this Honorable Court to enter an
Order . . .
```

See what I mean? It's Yoda-speak. After a while you get

the hang of it, though. When I showed it to Martinez, he begged me to add him, so then it was:

```
Come now the Plaintiffs, Atticus Tutwiler
Peale and Cinque Martinez Peale, acting
on their own behalf . . .
```

Okay, I know what you're thinking. Why does Atty have a boy's name? Well, long before I was born, Dad decided he wanted to name his first child after Atticus Finch, a lawyer in a famous book by some woman from Monroeville. His first child wasn't a boy. But Mom and Dad went with Atticus anyway.

And yes, Tutwiler is the name of a prison. It's also the name of Julia Tutwiler, a woman who tried to fix Alabama's prisons back in the 1800s. She also taught slaves to read, set up a college, and wrote Alabama's official state song. (Trust me, you've never heard it.)

I guess they could have named me Attica, the girl version of Atticus, but there's a prison with that name, too. Naming his daughter after two prisons was too weird even for Dad.

Hey, it could have been worse. Mom wanted to name me Podkayne. It's a long story.

```
. . . to enter an Order enjoining the
Strudwick County Animal Shelter to
postpone the destruction of the dog
known as 'Easy,' currently in their
custody.
```

"Enjoin" was a word I learned that day, and it's pretty useful. When a judge enjoins somebody, that basically means she orders them not to do something.

And that's how you start a legal brief. Then you list all the facts of the case, as you see them, in a numbered list, like this:

> 1) Easy is the name of a dog being held at the Strudwick County Animal Shelter.
>
> 2) Easy wears a tag that shows he has been immunized for rabies.
>
> 3) On June 29, a man showed up at the shelter claiming to be Easy's owner, and also claiming to have been bitten by the dog Easy.

And so on until you've told the whole story. Then you get into your argument. Again, you make your points in numbered paragraphs. And you have to quote big sections of the law and show where they appear in the law books.

> 20) According to Code of Alabama 3-7A-9, when a dog is accused of biting a human, 'if the owner of a dog, cat or ferret agrees in writing, or if ordered by the health officer, the animal shall be humanely destroyed immediately after exposure.' The man who claimed to own

```
Easy did not agree in writing, nor
would he even give his name when asked.
```

By the time I finished, I'd written fifteen pages of that stuff. It was dark outside. My fingers hurt from typing. And the strange thing was, it was so much easier than writing some dumb school paper on James K. Polk or the causes of the Civil War. I was writing something that mattered. Mimicking all that Yoda-talk is a small price to pay for saving a fuzzy, happy dog like Easy.

When I came out of my room Taleesa was in the kitchen, just closing her laptop.

"I'm hungry," I said.

"Me too," Taleesa said. "And no wonder. We've been working all day."

Working. I liked the sound of that.

When I'm not working, I play with dollhouses.

Not dolls. I hate dolls. It's the eyes, I think. Most dolls kind of stare into space like pretty little zombies. I know it's stupid, but I get the feeling that if I brought these little zombies into my bedroom, they'd stab me with little knives in the middle of the night. Give me a doll for Christmas and I'll blow it up at New Year's. That way I can honestly tell you I enjoyed my present.

Doll*houses* are different. Little plastic doors, each of them just like a real door on a real house, with a real shiny silver knob. A tiny perfect dining room table with perfect chairs. A kitchen where there's always a sticker of a perfect Thanksgiving turkey in the oven. I don't know anybody who doesn't like dollhouses, really, even though some folks won't admit it.

I have a whole neighborhood of them. Well, actually, Nutter McNutters does. He's a squirrel, a little toy squirrel I've had since I was about three years old. He used to be covered in bristly fuzz, most of which has rubbed off, but he still wears a little green vest and black tie that show he's successful in the squirrel world. He spends his time lounging around in his seven houses of various sizes, enjoying a life of luxury. He doesn't have adventures often, and I guess his life is kind of dull, if owning seven cars and spending a lot of time in the hot tub is dull.

McNutters was just settling into the jacuzzi with a martini that Saturday morning when Dad creaked the door open.

"It's time to revise," he said.

"I'm having a martini," I said in the voice of McNutters, which is high-pitched and stuffy.

"If you're going to take this brief to a judge, you need to read it again and correct your errors," he said. "That's always part of writing."

I sighed. "I'm having a martini."

"It's your case," he said. "If you want to win, you revise. Or you can leave it as it is and risk losing."

So of course I left McNutters with his martini and opened the laptop again. And was shocked at what I read:

```
Comes now Aticus tutwiler Peale and
Cinque Martinez Peale, acting their own
behalf, and asking this court . . .
```

I screamed and Taleesa flung the door open. I thrust the laptop at her.

"Taleesa, somebody got into my computer and put in a bunch of typos! It looks awful. Who would do that?"

Taleesa laughed. "It's the gremlins. It happens to me, too. Every time I write something, and then let it sit for a while, when I come back to read it the gremlins have messed it up."

I sighed. "I can't believe I didn't notice all those errors yesterday. How can I misspell my own name?"

Taleesa bent down and looked at the screen. "A-T-I-C-U-S. That's how. And there's only one cure for the gremlins. Sit down and read it three times, twice from front to back and once from back to front. And fix every error you see."

And that's how I spent a second day at the computer. Reading, fixing, rereading, looking stuff up in those musty old law books. By the time I was done, I felt like I knew Code of Alabama Title 3, Chapters 2 and 7, by heart. And I was sick to death of them. And I was hungry.

"I'm an idiot," I said at the dinner table. "The only thing I've proved is that a kid can't write a legal brief. I've spent my whole weekend at this, and I feel like I know less about law than when I started. It's hopeless."

Martinez gasped. "Don't say that. If you don't go to court, Easy will die. You're the opposite of hopeless. You're the only hope."

I tell you, sometimes I can't stand my brother. He's snide and selfish and immature. But when he said this, looking at me with big honest eyes I hadn't seen on him since kindergarten, I felt like I was about to burst with—I don't know, some sort of bursting emotion.

"This brief is actually pretty good," Dad said, flipping over pages on the table next to his plate. "You've got a chance."

That just made the bursting emotion bigger. Pride, I think it was.

"You should go to bed early tonight," Dad said. "You'll need your rest if you're going before the judge on Monday."

All through the writing, I'd never thought much about where this would end up—with me, in the courtroom, explaining my case to some grumpy old judge. It would be like going to the principal's office.

All of a sudden, my pride turned to fear.

4

"Okay. Steckley!" Judge Charles Grover said. "Is anybody here for Steckley? Paul Peale, is Steckley your client?"

Dad stood up.

"Sorry, Your Honor," he said. "Steckley's not mine."

"Well, he should be," the judge said. "Mr. Steckley's facing an assault charge, and his attorney isn't even here. I guess he'll sit in jail until somebody starts doing their job. Somebody find out who Mr. Steckley's attorney is and set him another court date. Who's next?"

Going to court isn't at all like what most people expect. On TV, there's a wise old judge in a courtroom with dark wood paneling, and people sit quietly watching while one witness after another takes the stand.

Strudwick County's courthouse looks more like someplace where old men get their hair cut. Green tile on the floors and halfway up the walls, a wall clock in every courtroom with no numbers, just hands. I hate those. Reading old clocks is hard enough as it is. And forget looking at your phone to see the time. A sign on every door read: "CELLULAR PHONES ARE NOT ALLOWED ANY-WHERE IN THE COURTHOUSE BY ORDER OF THE PRESIDING JUDGE."

There was nothing quiet or orderly about the place. There were rows of pews, like in a church, where about a dozen people just lounged around; an old guy in a Hawaiian shirt, a lady scribbling in a notebook, and a bunch of young guys with hunched shoulders, looking depressed. In the back of the room, men and women in business suits milled around, checking their watches, worriedly looking over big stacks of paper. Lawyers.

And there I was with them, in a black dress with big white flowers on it. The thing fit like a tent and it looked like something a woman would wear when she's about to have a baby. But I guess that's a grown-up look. It's hard for a twelve-year-old girl to find a dress that's right to wear in front of a judge.

"I feel like I'm wearing the living room curtains," I whispered to Dad.

"It's the best we could do," he whispered back. "It needs to be black. It doesn't need to be frilly."

"All right," said the judge. "Who's here for Barnett? Does Barnett have anybody here? Who's here for the state who can talk about the case?"

A lawyer standing near me raised his hand. "I am, Judge Grover."

"Well, get down here, prosecutor, and stop wasting this court's time," Grover barked.

The lawyer walked down the aisle and started explaining that Barnett was a guy awaiting trial on a drug charge, and that he was out on bail, and that the state wanted to keep custody of Barnett's cash and weapons until the trial.

"How's a guy going to get by in the world without his cash and his guns?" Grover said to the lawyer. I couldn't tell if he was serious or joking. "Give me one reason why a man who hasn't been convicted of anything shouldn't have his guns back."

The lawyer cleared his throat, "Well, Your Honor—"

"Quick now, I don't have all day," Grover snapped. "Oh, hell, since nobody's here for Barnett, I'll let you keep his guns. Next."

It was like that all morning. Grover called out for lawyers. Half of them weren't there. The other half got totally abused by Grover, who interrupted them, asked bizarre questions and then sent them off, telling them they needed to work harder and be smarter.

Soon I'd be up there myself.

"This guy is crazy," I whispered.

"He's being ornery on purpose," Dad whispered back. "He's just testing them to see how smart they are."

"He's mean."

"Don't let him scare you," Dad said. "Simple rules. Talk loud and slow. Say 'Your Honor' a lot. If you're angry when you say something, start out with 'with all due respect.'"

Loud and slow. Your Honor. All due respect. I repeated the rules to myself.

"Peale!" Judge Grover shouted. "Atticus T. Peale, representing himself? Paul Peale, is this a relative of yours? Why aren't you representing him?"

I took a step forward and raised my hand.

"I'm Atticus Peale," I said, loud and slow. "With all due respect, Your Honor, I am representing myself, and I can speak for myself."

Grover sat back, his eyebrows raised, as if I'd called him a name. *Oh no*, I thought. *I've lost him already.* But then I thought of what was at stake. The life of a sweet dog. I decided I'd just plow on, loud and slow.

As I marched down the aisle, I could feel every eye on me. When I got close to the judge's bench, Grover seemed to loom over me like a scary mall Santa.

"Atticus Tutwiler Peale," Grover said, peering at papers on his desk. "And this other character, Cinque Martinez Peale. Where is he?"

"Here, Your Honor," Martinez mumbled from the back of the room.

"Well, come on down here, Mr. Cinque." Turning to me, Grover said, "And you two are related how?"

"Brother and sister," I said. "It's in my brief."

"And Paul Peale is your father," Grover said. "Did he put you up to this? Paul Peale, is this some kind of a joke?"

Dad shrugged. "Believe me, Your Honor, I couldn't stop her from coming out here," he said. "She's very strong-willed."

That was a lie, of course. Dad was delighted that I was here. Why do parents lie to other grown-ups like that? It made me mad.

"Your Honor," I said. Loud and slow isn't hard when you're mad. "Your Honor, this is my case. This is my case, and I can speak for it."

Grover's eyes narrowed. His nostrils flared. "All right then, young lady, speak. I've read your brief. Tell me why this court should meddle in the affairs of the county animal shelter to save one dog. One dog that's already bitten someone."

I took a deep breath. Loud and slow. Especially important when you want to blurt something out.

"Your Honor," I said. "The law is pretty clear that a dog is considered dangerous only if it bites someone without being provoked. We don't know that Easy was unprovoked. Our only evidence of a bite came from a man who walked into the animal shelter with a gun, a man who refused to leave his name. A man who was rude to the point that I think we all were intimidated."

Grover grimaced at me, then leaned back in his chair and looked around the room. "The county!" he shouted. "Is there anybody here on behalf of Strudwick County? Someone to counter Miss Peale's claim?"

A gray-haired white guy strolled up the aisle with a briefcase in hand. He wore a pinstriped suit and had a deep, almost orange tan.

"The county's not contesting at this point, Your Honor," the man said. "I'm not convinced this little girl's claim is really going anywhere." Then he looked down at me with a big smile like a grandpa touring a kindergarten. "This is cute, honey," he said. "But you should wrap it up."

Honey, really! I stuck my hand out at him like a sudden karate chop. "I don't believe we've met."

"Backsley Graddoch," he said, as if it was some famous name. "County attorney for Strudwick County."

"Atticus T. Peale, attorney for myself."

"That's a pretty little dress you've got on there, young lady," Graddoch said.

"Thanks," I said. "I like your hands. They're really soft."

The crowd—lawyers, cops, guys from the jailhouse wearing orange jumpsuits—burst into laughter. Graddoch's big fake smile vanished and he glared down at me as if to say, "Okay, now it's really on."

Fine, I thought. *It's on.*

"Social hour's over," Judge Grover said. "Let's get back to the case. Miz Peale, tell me something. If an owner shows up at a shelter and says that's my dog, it bit me, go ahead and put it to sleep, why would the animal shelter not be within its rights to put the animal to sleep?"

"That's not what happened here, Your Honor," I said.

"I'm asking you a question," he said. "If we knew that was the owner, would the county have the right to put the dog down? Would it be obligated to?"

"I honestly don't know if they *have* to kill the dog, Your Honor," I said. "But you have to ask the question: Why would a dog bite its owner if it hasn't been provoked or abused? Especially a dog that comes to us with a bullet wound."

Graddoch stepped in front of me. "Really, Your Honor, isn't this too much trouble to take over one dog? How many dozens of dogs does the county put down every month? What if every one of those cases landed here? How could the shelter function?"

I stepped around Graddoch. "If every dog had someone on their side, we wouldn't have to put any of them down."

"Enough," said the judge. "I think I can rule on this right

here. Miz Peale, your case has some merit. If everyone is going to be treated equally under the law, then you've got as much right as anybody to ask the shelter not to put this dog down, at least for a couple of weeks."

My heart fluttered. But the judge kept on talking.

"But I'm afraid that's not what an animal shelter is for," the judge continued. "It's not a pet store. The right at issue is the public's right to be free of nuisance animals. Therefore, I'm going to let the shelter go ahead and put the dog down."

Oh, no. I thought. *I've lost already. Easy has lost.*

Graddoch looked down at me with a big gloaty smile. Some people just really like to win.

"Unless," the judge continued. "Unless you're equipped to keep the dog in the manner prescribed by law. There is a provision in law, wherein a dog that is known to bite can be kept alive—if the owner is willing to keep it locked in a cage, with no chance of escape, for the rest of its life. Assuming the owner will promise never to release it. I'd be willing to release the dog into the custody of someone who can secure it in that way. Are you equipped to take on a dog under those circumstances, Miz Peale?"

I hung my head. "No, Your Honor."

"Do you know anyone who is?"

I felt suddenly sick. So close to saving Easy, and I couldn't do it.

"I'll take the dog, Your Honor," said a voice behind me.

It was Miz Megg, standing in the back of the courtroom in her animal shelter uniform. Without waiting for the judge to ask, she walked up the aisle to stand beside me.

"I do have a pen, at home, that could hold such an

animal," she said. "It would be a hassle—I'd have to move my other dogs—but I could take it."

"Now Miz Megg," said the judge. "You of all people know you can't take every dog or cat home. You can't save them all."

"Well, I like the passion this young lady brings to this case," she said. "And I'll do it on one condition. Miss Peale and her brother have to promise to work for the shelter as volunteers, forty hours per week, for the rest of this summer."

I snatched her hand and shook it vigorously. "It's a deal."

"Now wait," said the judge. "There's another party to this agreement. Does young Mr. Peale also agree to work at the shelter?"

I knew the look on my brother's face. It was the *awwww, maaan* look.

"The whole summer?" he asked. But then he looked around, and saw everyone in the courtroom looking back. "I guess I don't have a choice."

"That's settled then," the judge said. "I can't say as I understand it. If you'd broken in and released the dog, you'd probably have gotten a lighter sentence. But if that's what you want, so be it. Now y'all clear out, so we can move on. Godbey. Is anybody here to represent Godbey?"

He didn't even bang the gavel.

Outside the courtroom, Dad gave me a big hug.

"I'm so proud of you," he said. "Of both of you. You stood your ground and you won your case."

I shook my head. "We didn't win. Easy's imprisoned for life. We just saved him from dying, but he isn't free."

"Trust me, that's a victory," Dad said. "Be proud."

Miss Megg walked up and patted me on the shoulder, a little too hard.

"Congratulations," she said. "I'll see you at eight tomorrow morning. And you, too, Martinez."

Martinez groaned. "Why the whole summer? Why forty hours a week?"

"Look, I can see that you love animals," Megg said. "There are a lot of people who think they love animals, but they don't put any work behind it. They think we're villains, because we put dogs down. Before you go flinging lawsuits around I want you to see what we do. I want you know how hard we work."

"I wasn't suing you, Miss Megg," I said. "Not personally. I know you love animals. I know you work hard."

"You think you know love," Megg said. "You think you know work. But you don't really know either until you've put in a forty-hour week." She looked up at Dad. "Eight o'clock."

Dad nodded, and Megg was gone.

5

I don't know what's sadder, a sad dog in a cage or a happy dog in a cage. The first time we visited Easy in his new home, he stood up with an eager look in his eye and wagged his tail as if we were about to throw him a ball. I knew he was expecting us to open the door and pet him. Thanks to the court order, that would never, ever happen.

He was imprisoned for life.

Not that it was bad, as prisons go. Megg's husband, who died years ago, once raised a dozen beagles in a big, broad pen behind their house. Later Megg turned the whole thing into a chicken run, adding a layer of chicken wire to the chain-link fence and even running chicken wire over the top. Over time, she'd added boards at the bottom, half-buried in the dirt, to keep foxes out. Now the big pen was occupied by Easy, who had his own little mini-yard to himself, with a doghouse and chew toys and dirt to run around in.

"Christmas will be hard," I said to Megg. "It could get cold, and Easy will have to be in here."

Megg nodded. "I agree. But a cold day on earth is better than a grave. And just think of all the strays that are out there every Christmas."

Megg let us come up to her house for lunch on our first day of work at the shelter. Martinez wanted to get a picture of Easy in his new home. It's hard, but if you hold your phone right up to the wire you can get a shot of a caged animal without any bars in the way. When Martinez finally got a good shot of Easy, his face lit up with joy, like he only just then realized we'd saved his life. I think that for Martinez, things aren't really real until you see them on a screen.

I'm not like that. Pictures make me sad. Before Megg sat us down to lunch, she showed us around her house, which was full of photos of her family. Megg and her long-gone husband, both in their Navy uniforms. Their daughter, who was in the Coast Guard in Galveston. Countless beloved dogs that were now in doggie heaven.

"Don't they make you sad, all those pictures?" I asked over lunch. I realized almost immediately that maybe it wasn't the nicest thing to say, but Megg didn't seem to mind.

"Taking care of others is the cure for all sadness," she said, matter-of-factly. "Changing diapers, cleaning cages, even fixing lunch for you two." She reached over the table and poured more tea into my sweating glass.

"I have pictures of my mom, but I never look at them," I blurted out. Why was I talking about this, I wondered? "Not Taleesa, but my mom who died."

Megg nodded. "Well, pictures can be sad," she said. "I bet

she was pretty. Would you mind showing me one of those photos sometime?"

I was about to say that I didn't have any on with me, when Martinez butted in. "I've got one in my phone. I asked Dad to text it to me." He looked at me. "What? She's my mom, too. She's my mom as much as my mom is your mom."

I wasn't going to argue. Martinez pulled up the photo. A tall, pale woman with limp, strawberry-blonde hair.

"What's that uniform she's wearing?" Megg asked.

"Starfleet," I said. "She made it herself. She was a huge science fiction fan. She was writing a book about the history of science fiction, for her PhD, when she died."

"Beautiful," Megg said. "What was her name?"

"Ilia Woodley," I said. "Her parents named her Magnolia, but she didn't like that, so she had it changed to Ilia. Ilia's the name of the bald chick in the first *Star Trek* movie."

Megg just smiled warmly. Not a condescending smile. I knew right then that I liked her a whole lot. Life is hard when you live in a small town where most people think your dead mom was crazy.

"I take after her," Martinez said. "I'm the science fiction fan in the family."

I shook my head. "Martinez, you can't take after her because she's not . . ." I looked down into my little brother's earnest face. "Oh, never mind. She can be your mom, too."

"You know," Megg said. "In Tibet, they believe that everybody comes back after death as something else. Some other animal. And since everybody's constantly coming back, it's a safe assumption that everyone you meet was once your mother in some past life. Even the spider crawling across the floor."

Martinez laughed. "I'm your mother, Miz Megg."

"And I thank you for mothering me," Megg said. "Now, let's get back to work."

I learned a lot about poop during that first week. If Animal Shelter were a video game on your phone, you'd see a dozen dogs on a screen and you'd rush back and forth trying to feed each one of them when they're hungry and play with them when they're sad. When you make them happy, a little heart would appear over their heads.

In real life, something else appears, something that you don't usually see in a video game. And you have to clean it up. If the dog poops outside in the play yard, you have to scoop it up and throw it away. If they poop in the cage, you have to go in and get it. By the end of the first week, I was cleaning poop in my dreams. Of course, I was also seeing dog faces: Labradors, Brittanies, beagles all looking up at me expectantly, tails wagging.

I didn't do cat poop. On our first day, Megg told us about something called toxoplasma, a germ that gets transmitted through cat poop. Some people worry that it can make you crazy; mice who've been infected with it will stand up and fight cats instead of running away. As soon as he heard about that, Martinez demanded to work in the cat room. "I want to get the supermouse germ," he said.

So this was our work. Scooping poop, pouring food, taking dogs out of cages one at a time to go to the play yard, cleaning up with bleach. After a while, bleach, poop, and dog all kind of smelled the same to me. And I could sit right there among the dog cages, odor and all, and eat the brown-bag lunch Taleesa packed for me.

"I feel like a guy in a hard hat," I said. "Sitting on a girder and eating out of a metal lunch box. So much work. So hungry."

Martinez, sitting beside me, just nodded. Then, through a mouthful of baloney sandwich: "Hey look." He showed me his phone. "We're in the newspaper."

I grabbed the phone. It was a story in the Houmahatchee *Herald.*

KID LAWYERS DEFEND DOG

Two young people from Houmahatchee came to the rescue of a canine defendant in Strudwick County Circuit Court Monday, court documents show.

Atticus Peale, 12, and her nine-year-old brother Cinque filed an emergency legal brief Monday morning appealing for a stay of execution for Easy, a stray dog accused of biting a man.

Easy was picked up by county animal control officers last week, court records show. Later that afternoon, a man showed up at the county animal shelter claiming the dog bit him. A police report says the man wouldn't tell shelter workers his name, acted in a belligerent manner, and was carrying a handgun.

The Peale children, acting as their own lawyers, filed a motion arguing that as potential adopters of the dog, they had a right to demand more time before Easy is put to sleep. Dogs that bite are typically put down as soon as drugs are available to do so. The children also argued that Easy had wounds that showed the dog may have been provoked.

Judge Charles Grover said he doesn't comment on cases he's heard, though he remarked that Atticus Peale, known by the nickname "Atty," was able to hold her own against County Attorney Backsley Graddoch in courtroom debate.

"She'll make a fine lawyer someday, I'm sure," he said.

The case was settled when an animal shelter employee promised to take the dog in and keep it locked in a secure pen for life.

Attempts to reach the Peales for comment were unsuccessful.

—Rickie Braxton, *Herald* staff reporter

"Oh my lands," I said. Which is something I never say. The story made me nervous, but I laughed. "Martinez, how on earth did you find this?"

"I have Google News set up to give me an alert when I'm mentioned in the news," he said. "That way, when I become famous, I'll know what they're saying about me."

Ah, Martinez. I just shook my head. Then I had a thought, and dug my own phone out of my pocket. Yes, there was a missed call from a 251 number that must have been the Houmahatchee *Herald*. And a voice mail from a lady named Rickie.

"Hey," Martinez said. "I just did a search for you. And here's another story. This one's from London."

"What? There's a London, Alabama?"

"London, England, dummy." He handed me the phone.

This one was from a newspaper called the *Daily Royal Post*.

```
ATTY AT LAW: Twelve-year-old flouts
Alabama statute, becomes lawyer for
dogs
   A preteen girl with an auspicious
name is defying the law in the U.S.
state of Alabama to defend dogs in
court.
   Atticus Peale, 12, went to court in
the tiny town of Houmahatchee to defend
a dog named Easy from death.
   The dog stood accused of biting
a local resident, but young Atticus
```

faced off in court against a veteran
barrister, Strudwick County Attorney
Backsley Graddoch, to defend the
animal. Her advocacy got Easy a
sentence of life in a cage, instead of
death.

The local Houmahatchee *Herald* quoted
judge Charles Grover as saying the
girl trounced Graddoch in courtroom
arguments, calling her a "fine lawyer."

The preteen may have defied state
law in order to become a lawyer for
animals. The state bar association says
she's not licensed as an attorney in
Alabama, and that it would likely be
impossible for a child to be admitted
to law school in the state.

Graddoch told the *Royal Post* that
he'd call for an investigation into the
young barrister's qualifications.

"If it's true, as you say, that she's
holding herself out as a lawyer, that
would be a violation of the law," he
said. "Under Section 34-3-1 of the
Alabama Code, it's a misdemeanor to
falsely claim that you're a lawyer."

That misdemeanor is punishable by
up to six months in jail, Graddoch
said. Alabama's jails are among the
most brutal in the United States, and

Alabama inmates as young as 14 have
been sent to adult prisons.

A young girl couldn't pick a tougher
lawyer to fight. Graddoch, 62, is a
former candidate for the Alabama
Supreme Court known for waging one
of the nastiest campaigns in recent
Alabama history. That campaign included
a widely circulated advertisement that
seemed to claim that his opponent,
Michael Boudreaux, was a convicted
murderer. In fact, that murder was
committed by another man by the same
name.

Graddoch lost his race by just a few
hundred votes.

Ever climb up a really tall ladder and then realize you're
afraid to climb back down? That's how I felt, suddenly.

Six months in grown-up prison! Was that really possible?

"What are they even talking about?" I said. "I never pretended to be an actual lawyer, and Graddoch knows that!
And this paper in London, they didn't even try to call me
for a response."

"Look on the bright side," Martinez said. "You're in
newspapers in two countries, so you're officially WORLD
FAMOUS. You should start printing and selling T-shirts.
'Atty at Law.' That would look good on a shirt."

"Absolutely not," I said. "Stop it. You're looking up T-shirt
companies right now, aren't you? Stop it."

Martinez set the phone down, picked up the rest of his sandwich. "You're no fun." Then, after a few bites: "Hey, did you know that when you're smelling cat poop, it's because microscopic particles of cat poop are going up into your nose and being absorbed into your body?"

I kept eating. Already a hardened poop veteran.

Just then, Megg gently opened the door and looked at us like a mom checking on a sick kid. "Atty, Martinez? We have a visitor for you."

Out at the front desk stood a cop. A sheriff's deputy, actually. They're the ones in the tan uniforms who patrol the country roads. A white guy with a great tan and thick dark hair, cropped short. This guy had real muscles: on the muscle scale, he was somewhere between a high school coach and an action figure.

"Atticus Peale, Martinez Peale?" he asked. "Chief Deputy Troy Butler. I'd like to have a word with you."

His hand, when I shook it, was hard as a rock. The smell of his cologne for some reason had me imagining his wife, straightening his badge for him before he left for work.

"Miss Peale, we've heard reports that you've claimed you're an attorney when you're not," he said. "I'd like to talk to you for a bit and get your side of the story."

I know you're supposed to be nice to the police. Taleesa has told Martinez a thousand times that talking back to them can get you in bigger trouble than you ever imagined. But I guess I'm a hothead.

"There's no sides to the story, officer," I said. "There are facts. The fact is, I went to court on my own behalf. There's nothing illegal about that. Even for a kid."

He opened a little pouch on his utility belt and pulled out a printout of the London newspaper story. "This article says otherwise," he said. "And we've had a report from a citizen who's concerned that you may be defrauding the public by holding yourself out as a licensed attorney."

He held the paper out as if he expected me to take it.

"I've read it," I said. "The story's wrong. Now this concerned citizen: would his initials happen to be B.G.?"

The deputy didn't flinch, didn't blink.

"I'm not at liberty to reveal that information, Miss Peale." Finally, he seemed to relax a bit. "Look, Miss Peale, I'm not . . . Hey, can I call you Atty?"

"If I can call you . . . whatever your first name is." I hadn't forgotten, really.

"Okay, Atty, you can call me Troy. Look, I don't really intend to arrest you or put you in jail or anything, unless the law absolutely requires me to do it. I've never seen a case like this. But I have to investigate this complaint. It's my job."

"All you have to do is go to the courthouse and get my brief—our brief—and you'll see that the charge is false. It's that simple."

"Can you provide me with a copy of the brief, Atty?" he asked.

I could hardly even hear him. Now that he was talking to me like a human being, I could see that his eyes were a deep, dark brown. He already had some dark stubble growing in even though he'd probably shaved that morning.

I've been told I'm a bit of a late bloomer, when it comes to boys and all that. I think Taleesa is starting to wonder why I don't show a lot of interest in some of the things other girls my age are interested in.

I'm not interested in boys. Or in girls, either. Men and women interest me, in that way, but only a little. One time Taleesa and I sat and watched a video of Prince William and Princess Kate saying their wedding vows in this big, beautiful British church, and it gave me this odd feeling of warm yearning. Up to that point, that was the closest I'd ever come to giggling at a boy.

But here I was, standing in front of this Troy character, and inside, I'm giggling.

"You're a despicable human being," I told him. "You're here to arrest a little girl, based on something you read in a foreign newspaper. Why don't you trust what you read in your own town's newspaper? Why don't you go to the court and look for yourself?"

Everybody stood silent and shocked for a moment. "Despicable" was too much, I knew. His stubble threw me off.

"You know, Miss Peale, you have a point," he said. "I've got your statement, and it's my job, not yours, to do the investigation. So I thank you for your time, and I'll get back in touch."

Again the handshake. He tipped an invisible hat to Megg and left.

Megg craned her head to watch him go. Then she turned to me with a twinkle in her eye.

"Pretty dreamy, huh?" she said.

I blushed. And crossed my arms.

"If you like that sort of thing," I said. "He's not exactly Prince William."

Just then my cell phone quivered in my pocket. A text from Dad.

TALEESA'S STILL IN ATMORE WORKING ON HER STORY. I'LL PICK YOU UP AT 3.

I kept up the bluster for the rest of the day, but I can tell you now that inside, I was scared. If you've ever been in this kind of trouble, threatened with actual jail, you know how scary it can be. How could I tell Dad? *Did* I break the law and not know it? How would I survive in kids' jail—a juvenile detention center or whatever—surrounded by a bunch of mean girls and guards and counselors who treat me like I have an illness? My cell phone vibrated again and again—a message from Dad about dinner, some dumb e-mail ads—and I felt a little jolt of fear with each one.

"No time to fret," Megg said. "There's work to do. It's resupply day. Some volunteers have been down to the co-op to pick up the week's litter and food. You two will need to help unload the truck. The fifty-pound bags are too big for you, but there are usually smaller bags of cat food."

Martinez groaned. "I didn't realize working was so much work. How do grown-ups do this all day?"

Megg laughed. "Believe me, there's tougher work than this. When you're done, you can play with the cats. I've got other work going on, something I didn't have time to do yesterday because we were in court, and I'll be out of touch for a while."

I guess I'm just too curious. "What other work?" I asked. "Anything fun?"

Megg sighed. "I was going to try not to bring it up. But you might as well know. You already do know. You know we have to put down some of the animals from time to time. They've been here too long, or they're sick, we need to make room for more. Well, now is the time. It always rips me up. No need for you to have to be involved. Not this early in your work here."

Oh god. I knew about the walk down the hall, the white table, the needle they use to put the dogs to sleep. To kill them. But like everybody else in the world, I chose not to think much about it. Now Megg herself was going to kill those dogs.

"How many?" I asked.

"Twenty-five this month," she said. "A small number, for summer."

"How can you possibly . . . how do you pick them out?" I said.

"I've done it already," she said. "The little pink tags that were on some of the cages this morning? They're the ones."

I immediately thought of Frankie. A tangle-haired mutt I'd played with that morning. He looked like Benji, the dog from that old movie, but skinnier, with a dirty, mangy look that no amount of care and brushing seemed to fix. But his eyes were wise and sad and patient. When I looked into those eyes, I pictured an old family dog who was good with toddlers.

His cage had a pink tag.

I didn't stop to think. I ran out of the room to Frankie's cage. I turned to face Megg, and laced my fingers in the wire of the cage door. "I won't let you."

Megg wiped away a tear. "You may not believe it, Atty, but I hate it as much as you do. It's just something we have to do."

I could feel Frankie's warm tongue licking my fingers.

"You don't have to do it to *this* dog. This dog is adoptable. This dog, all these dogs and cats, they need someone to speak up for them. Individually. They need a lawyer. How can you kill a dog like this, without even giving him a hearing?"

Megg didn't say anything. She just gave me a sad, anguished look that reminded me of the hallway in her house, full of photos of dead pets and relatives.

"Megg," I said. "Let me be the lawyer for these animals. Every one of them needs an advocate. Somebody to make their case before you do this."

Megg snatched the pink tag off Frankie's cage. "Here," she said. "You want to save Frankie? Then pick another dog to take his place. Go ahead."

I looked up and down the rows of cages. Bert the beagle. Harriet the sheepdog. Every one a dog we knew, all of them completely unaware that I had the power of life or death over them.

"These dogs do need an advocate," Megg said. "But I'm not the judge you need to make your case with. There are enough homes out there for all of these animals, even in a poor county like Strudwick. There are people who sell puppies at fruit stands by the road. At flea markets, at pet stores. There are people who want a dog and never got around to getting one. Those are the people who need to hear Frankie's case. The people who could come in here and adopt Frankie, but haven't."

All was grim and silent for a moment. Megg and I stared at each other. Martinez, as he often does in moments of stress, stared at his phone.

"Cat videos," he said calmly.

I shook my head. "What?"

"Cat videos. They're the most popular thing on the Internet. People post little kitten videos all the time on their sites just to get people to visit, even if it's a site about bridges or trains or something. We could make cute videos about each animal. And post them, and invite people to come adopt them."

Megg nodded. "I've considered that before. Honestly, I don't know that it would work here. There are a lot of people in Strudwick County who still don't have the Internet."

"Why do we care where the kittens and puppies go?" Martinez said. "If somebody in Montgomery wants to drive down to Houmahatchee and adopt a kitten, the kitten's still adopted. Tell the whole world about our pets."

Megg grinned. "That's pretty brilliant," she said. "You know, the *Herald* used to have a column where they'd show one of our animals in the paper every week, with a little write-up. But then they cut back on staff and they stopped doing it. Maybe if you and Atty write a column and send it to them every week, they'll publish it again. So there we get the local audience, too."

My fingers relaxed on the cage, just a bit. "All this doesn't save Frankie."

"Maybe it saves the next Frankie, though," Megg said.

Frankie licked my fingers again. I let go of the wire. "I need to say goodbye," I said.

Megg opened the cage. I kneeled. Frankie came up to me with expectant eyes, as if he was sure I held a treat in my hand. I hugged him.

"Goodbye, Frankie," I said. "We love you, and we will always love you. I hope there's some way you can know that."

We heard a honk outside. Megg wiped away more tears.

"Caring for others is the cure for all sadness," she said. "The truck is here. Let's get back to work."

6

B y the time Dad pulled up, Martinez and I had it all
worked out. We'd set up an online video channel called
Strudwick Puppy and Kitten Rescue. We'd start with the
cutest, smallest animals, playing with fuzzy balls. Every
video would have the address and phone number of the
county animal shelter at the end, with directions on how
to get there from Atlanta, Montgomery, and Panama City.
A Twitter feed and Facebook page with links to the videos.
If it caught on, we'd start posting videos of the older, scruff-
ier-looking dogs, too.

"What if we put up a video of a dog and he doesn't get
adopted?" Martinez asked. "What if he, you know, turns
out like Frankie? Do we keep the video up? That would be
creepy."

"Take it down," I said. "If people want cute puppy videos,
they need to support cute puppies. And if people ask, we'll
tell them that."

I'd forgotten all about my other troubles until Dad walked into the animal shelter.

"Come on, Atty, Martinez," he said. "We're going to jail."

I should have told Dad right then and there about the visit from the sheriff's deputy. I didn't.

As it turns out, we weren't going to jail because of me. Dad had a new case, a big one, and he needed to meet his client at the jail.

"Capital murder," Dad said. "You know what capital murder is?"

I couldn't say anything. The idea that I too could go to jail for something filled me with a kind of icy fear. What was this feeling, exactly? Shame?

"So he shot someone in Montgomery?" Martinez asked. "That's the capital."

"Capital murder is the most severe murder charge you can face," Dad said. "If convicted, you could face the death penalty. And you won't believe who the defendant is. The last person you'd suspect of murder."

"Mom? You?" Martinez asked. "Atty?"

"Shut up, Martinez," I snapped.

Dad shook his head.

"Jethro Gersham," he said. "You know. Mister Jethro from the Speedy Queen. What was it you used to call him? Matterfike?"

Jethro Gersham lived in a peeling-paint house near the Speedy Queen milkshake place on Galvez Road. Nobody knew exactly how old he was, but he sure seemed old. He'd been on Social Security for as long as anybody could remember, and he'd worked for decades as a farmhand harvesting shade tobacco in Florida. Dad said he must have been retired a while, because the tobacco farms in the Panhandle died out years ago. Yet Jethro was tall and slim and nimble and could be seen walking down the highway— always in tennis shoes and jeans and a windbreaker—on the coldest of nights and the hottest of days. When people asked Jethro how old he actually was, he'd just laugh and say that black don't crack. But to me he seemed totally cracked. With his cloudy right eye, close-shaved white hair, and the deep grooves in his cheeks, he seemed to me like he was made out of wood or rock, cracked again and again by the hot sun until nothing could really hurt him.

If you stopped for a cone at the Speedy Queen, there was a good chance you'd run into him in the parking lot. He'd ask where you're headed. You'd tell him, and ask if he needed a ride.

"As a matter of fact, I do," he always said. He said "matter of fact" a lot. Thus the nickname Martinez and I always used behind his back. Matterfike this and matterfike that.

Strudwick County fathers always lectured their daughters about how you never, ever, ever pick up a hitchhiker, because they're dangerous. They had to preach extra hard, because in reality everybody made an exception for Mr. Jethro. So the notion of Jethro actually killing somebody really was a shocker. I could remember him sitting beside me in the car when I was seven, holding Nutter McNutters between his thumb and forefinger and examining the toy squirrel with his good eye, before smiling and handing him back to me.

"Jeez, Dad," I said. "Who did he kill? How?"

"Well, he's *alleged* to have killed J. D. Ambrose, the guy who owns—well, owned—the pawnshop at the corner of Iberville and Galvez," Dad said. "They found Jethro with a gun, and with a $225,000 lottery ticket that apparently belonged to Ambrose. Which makes for a tough case."

In case you've never been to a pawnshop, here's how it works. If you're short on money, you take some of your stuff—maybe a TV or radio—and sort of sell it to the pawnshop. The shop gives you a little money, say $15 for a TV, and they put your TV out on the shelves for other people to buy, for maybe $30 or $40. If you can scrape up the money to buy your TV from the pawnshop before someone else buys it, you can get it back. Otherwise, you've lost your TV. It's kind of like taking out a loan, but easier, and I guess sadder sometimes. I know about pawnshops because sometimes stolen stuff turns up there, and the pawnshop owner winds up calling my dad to defend him on a stolen property charge.

"The police say Jethro hocked his pistol at Ambrose's shop a while ago," Dad said. "It was looking like he wouldn't get it back. Early last week, other customers saw him arguing loudly with Ambrose at the pawnshop, saying God would punish Ambrose for being a crook. A couple of days later, a customer comes in and finds Ambrose dead in the back office, shot with a .38 pistol. The police look through Ambrose's cell phone and find that Jethro's the last person Ambrose called. They pick up Jethro to talk to him, and Jethro admits he was there, and that he picked up the pistol, and that Ambrose simply gave him back the pistol because he was feeling generous because he'd just won the lottery."

"Wait," I said. "I thought you said they caught Jethro with a lottery ticket in his pocket."

"Yep. That's the problem," Dad said. "The bullet in Ambrose is from the gun Jethro was carrying. The ticket is a winner—$225,000 in Florida's Fantasy Five."

I shook my head. "So he's guilty, then. He just shot Ambrose and took the ticket." For a while I watched the landscape roll by and tried to imagine how the man who held Nutter McNutters in his hand could also be a killer.

"I can't believe it," I said finally. "He sat right in this car with us, and he's a killer, I can't believe it."

"Put a pin in that thought, Atty," Dad said. "Keep that thought hanging there, where you can see it. Because nobody's guilty until they're proven guilty. And I'm going to be the one arguing that he's not guilty."

I could feel Martinez kicking the back of the car seat, the way he does when he wants attention.

"I just realized something, Dad," he said. "If you're a lawyer for people who are accused of crimes, if that's all you do, then there are times when you're going to defend people who have really done the crime. I mean, *somebody* killed Ambrose, and whoever did it, they're going to have a lawyer. How can you defend someone who killed someone?"

"Easy," Dad said. "Because I believe that everybody deserves to have an advocate. Every human being, no matter what they've done, needs one person on their side, to tell the story from their point of view. To make sure that justice is really done."

"Come on, Dad," Martinez said. "Even a murderer?"

"Even a guilty person deserves a day in court," he said.

"Suppose you got into a fight at school. Somebody came up to you and threw the first punch, and you punched back. What would happen to you?"

"Well, sheesh," Martinez said. "I'd get kicked out of school. Everybody knows that."

"Even if you didn't start it?" Dad said.

"Of course," Martinez said, as if Dad was a complete dummy. "It's zero tolerance. The teachers talk about it all the time."

"But what if somebody was there to speak for you?" Dad asked. "To say, Martinez is actually the victim, and the other guy attacked him?"

Martinez shrugged. "I don't know. I don't get in fights. I've never even thought about it. You know that."

"That's good," Dad said. "But I think you see what I mean. Think of some other thing. Talking in class, passing notes, running in the hall. Haven't you ever gotten into trouble in school?"

I put my hand up, so quickly that Dad flinched.

"Don't answer that, Martinez," I said. "Dad, I don't see how this is relevant to the conversation."

My dad looked at me with a smile.

"You're a born lawyer, Atty."

The Strudwick County Jail creeps me out. It's not creepy the way jails are creepy on TV. There are no bars on any of the doors. It's not a dimly lit row of cells where the light of the setting sun climbs across the wall and some guy plays the harmonica.

Think instead of a big flat building like some old high

school. Inside, bright fluorescent light like a convenience store. Tan cinder-block walls and clerks who talk to you through a thick glass window. Sit in the waiting room, and you hear big steel doors opening and closing, and radios squawking about "B Pod open" and "B Pod closed" and so on. Outside, behind a tall fence with barbed wire at the top, guys in orange jumpsuits lounge around on picnic tables and stroll around a basketball court. Most of them look sad and tired. A few of them look scary. It's like a giant version of the principal's office at school, except people stay there for months.

I'd been here a couple of times before, with Dad, just to pick up paperwork. One time I held a baby for a woman who was waiting to visit her husband. She had two other kids, toddlers, running all over the waiting room. She had baby-barf stains all over her shirt and looked like she could use some sleep.

Martinez, however, had never been to the jail. He was excited.

"The slammer," he whispered. "I always wondered what it looks like in here."

The waiting room was empty this time. We went up to the little thick-glass window and Dad talked to the woman on the other side.

"I'm here to see Jethro Gersham. I've been appointed to represent him," Dad said. "And if it's okay, my kids are going to wait here in the lobby."

As he spoke, one of the big metal doors opened, and out came two sheriff's deputies in their tan uniforms. My heart almost stopped. Neither of them was Troy Butler—but what if Troy Butler was here? What if he came through the lobby while we were waiting for Dad? What if he ran into Dad in the jail and told him how he'd come to talk to me earlier today? The thought made me feel sick. I tugged on Dad's sleeve.

"Dad, we need to go in with you," I said.

"What?" he said. "No way. This is a jail, and I'm having a conference with a client. It's confidential."

"We're not staying alone here at the jail," I said. "It's creepy. And we're just kids. I'd feel safer with you."

All lies. Except there was a real chance Dad would run into Troy Butler here, and if that happened, I wanted to be there, too. Maybe I could steer Dad away from talking to the deputy. Maybe I could . . . I don't know. When you decide you feel guilty about something, when you decide to hide something, all logic goes out the window.

"What about you, Martinez?" Dad said. "Are you nervous here in the lobby?"

"Oh, Dad, I'm *so scared* here in the lobby," he said. "I'd rather be with you."

When Dad turned back to the woman in the window, Martinez looked at me with an openmouthed face of joy.

"You're such a bad actor," I whispered.

"He bought it," Martinez whispered back.

And so we went in. Radio squawks, a buzz, and the sound of a big metal door opening. Into a little windowless room with one bare table. A deputy—thank goodness, not Troy Butler—walked in with Jethro.

He didn't look like the same person we knew. He wasn't just handcuffed; he had chains on his arms, chains that attached to a set of chains on his legs, so he could walk only in a shuffle. Later I realized that his orange jail jumpsuit was way too big for him; they probably didn't have the right size for a tall, skinny guy, so he was wearing a prison suit big enough for a football player. He almost tripped himself up, waving at us excitedly.

"Hey!" he said to me. "I know you! You the girl with the squirrel toy."

I laughed. "I'm surprised you remembered."

"Matter of fact, a guy don't forget a white girl with a black brother," he said. "You don't see that every day in Houma-hatchee, matter of fact."

Dad motioned to the deputy. "Before you go, can you take the chains off? He's got some things to sign."

"No sir," the deputy said. "He's a capital murder suspect. And there are children here."

"He's my friend, and he's innocent. And anyway, you'll be just outside the door," Dad said.

"We'll scream in agony if we need you," Martinez said. Dad glared at him; I punched Martinez on the arm.

"He can sign with the chains on," the deputy said. "I'll be right outside."

We all sat down at the table. Dad took a bunch of papers out of his briefcase and spread them out.

"Here's some paperwork you'll need to sign so I can take you on as attorney," he said. "We'll need to do this before we get started. Normally, I'd talk to you about the circumstances of the case, but we're not alone and we need confidentiality when we discuss those matters."

"I got nothing to hide. I told the cops. He give me back

my gun, and he even give me a ticket for it, and that's all I know," Jethro said. "I didn't kill nobody. Matter of fact."

Dad held up a hand. "That's fine, we can talk about all of that later."

But it wasn't fine with me. "You're saying he gave you a lottery ticket? He just gave it to you?"

"Atty, hush," Dad said. "You're not supposed to—"

"He give me a ticket, just like you get at the store when you buy something," Jethro said. "I always take the ticket so they can't say I shoplifted."

"You mean a receipt," I said. "He gave you a receipt and the gun."

"Atty, you're going to get me in trouble here," Dad said. "These are things that are between me and Mr. Gersham."

I leaned in. I couldn't help myself. "*Who* gave you the receipt? Ambrose? The man who was shot?"

"No, some other guy," Jethro said. "Guy in a red ball cap."

"That's it, Atty. One more word and I'm sending you to the lobby." Dad pushed some papers and a pen toward Jethro. "You'll want to read and sign these."

"I don't need to read them," Jethro said. "You tell me what's in there."

"It gives me permission to be your attorney," Dad said. "But you should read it on your own before you sign, and ask any questions you need to ask. I insist."

Jethro bent down close to the page, turning his non-cloudy eye toward the words, and hummed to himself as he looked it over.

While he read, I quietly slipped another paper off the desk. It was what they call the indictment, the list of charges against Jethro. And attached to it was a photocopy of Exhibit A—the lottery ticket that was found on Jethro.

It was clear from the copy that the lotto ticket was stapled to something. On the second page of Exhibit A was a photocopy of the thing that was stapled to the front of the lottery ticket: a slip of paper with a bunch of gobbledygook printed on it:

1234567
wefpoj
wf;l
qpweodfk
pfoj
'sdlfkef
12345

Weird, I thought. What was that for?

Jethro signed the papers and we were done, for now. More buzzes, more squawks and we were out in the lobby of the jail. Almost home free.

But as Dad stopped at the window to sign us out, I felt someone tapping me lightly on the shoulder. I looked up to see Backsley Graddoch, the county attorney.

"Well, Ms. Peale, what brings a young girl like you to the county jail?" he asked with a grin.

"It's confidential," I said firmly.

Dad turned and shook Graddoch's hand. "Hey, Backsley, good to see you. Yeah, I've been appointed on the Ambrose case. We have first appearance tomorrow."

"So you were here meeting your client?" Graddoch said.

He was asking Dad, I guess, but he was looking straight at me. "Good of you to bring the kids along."

Dad nodded. "So what brings you here, Backsley?"

Graddoch laughed. "Oh, nothing, really. I'm here to meet a deputy, Troy Butler. You've probably heard why already."

"No," Dad said. "Fill me in."

"It's confidential," Graddoch said, winking at me. "But the rumor mill works fast. You'll find out soon enough."

Flags are popular in Strudwick County. Alabama and Auburn football flags, Marine Corps flags, the Confederate battle flag, and of course the American flag. Probably every third house has some banner hanging off the porch, or on a pole in the yard.

And lots of them are faded and tattered. I've always wondered about that. If you're patriotic enough to hang up the American flag, why do you leave it when it's all ragged and faded into pink and light blue?

As I watched trailers and porches and flags whiz past on the way home, I realized I already knew why. It was guilt. You realize the flag's a little faded, and it fills you with embarrassment. So you ignore it. Weeks later, the flag is starting to look tattered. More guilt. So you ignore it even harder. Soon everyone driving by knows your flag is ragged and tacky. But when you look at it, the guilt pulls at you like the gravity on the surface of Jupiter. You can't lift an arm to take the flag down.

That's how I felt about the visit from Deputy Troy Butler. I knew I'd done nothing criminal, and I knew Graddoch's charge was bogus. Why didn't I just tell Dad as soon as I saw him? For some reason I didn't, and that wasn't like me. I'm not a sneak; in my family, we don't keep secrets.

But I did keep a secret, and the longer I kept it, the harder it pulled at me. The more I worried about getting into trouble—the more I wanted assurance from Dad that everything was okay—the less inclined I felt to tell him. By the time we got home, I decided that I'd never tell Dad.

I guess we all want to look better than we are. Even when we're innocent. I wondered how many people, accused of a crime, lied about it not because they feared jail, but just because they didn't want to look so bad.

The thought kept me quiet all the way to dinnertime. Frozen pizza, Dad's go-to when Taleesa is out of town.

"So who's the man in the red ball cap, then?" I asked. "If he exists, we can find him."

"He exists," Dad said, with an it's-my-client certainty. "I just haven't found him yet. Ambrose, the store owner, had a partner, who runs the store now. But the partner has an alibi. He was fishing all day at Lake Rufus King. He's got receipts to prove it, from the marina where he put his boat in."

Fishing's a big thing in Strudwick County. The whole state of Alabama is covered in lakes named after stodgy old white guys, lakes that were created like a hundred years ago when they dammed up the rivers. Without the Rufus King Dam, there wouldn't be anything in Strudwick County but pine plantations and Red Creek. If you stop up the river with a dam, of course, all the water piles up on one side and makes a lake. Dad said Lake Rufus King was probably only four feet deep, but old guys always make a big deal about buying a house out there and living the good life. And on the other side of the dam, there's just a trickle of a river, a pile of gray rocks on the creek bank where people fish, and some scraggly forest where nobody lives, I guess because it's not safe to be there when they open the dam up and let water out. Taleesa says Alabama is all about dams. Everywhere you look, she says, they've drawn a line and put all the good stuff on one side.

"Did the cops even look for Red Hat Man?" I asked.

"It's our job to find him, I guess," Dad said. "And to be clear, by *our* job I mean *my* job. You've got your own causes to work on. I'm thinking we could both get into hot water if you meddle in my work."

I gulped, nervous.

But I still wanted to know who Red Hat Man was.

Sleep is great when you're feeling anxious. I was dreaming that I was at the helm of a starship. My mom, Ilia, was there, in a Starfleet uniform like in her picture. Taleesa and Miz Megg were working at a computer panel. And Mario, from the video game, was in the back of the room, on hands and knees, rolling dice on the floor. And then everything shook.

I opened my eyes. It was Martinez.

"It's a code," my brother said. He was holding his phone, a square of painful light.

"What on earth?"

"That piece of paper that was stapled to the lottery ticket. I took a picture of it." He showed me the photo on the phone.

"Ugh, that's bright," I said. "Why did you take a picture? I'm pretty sure that's evidence. I don't know if it's something we're allowed to take a picture of."

"This is the key to the case," Martinez said. "It isn't just nonsense. There are repeating letters, like words. It's a code and I'm going to crack it. And then I'll solve the case."

"What are you talking about? Why would Red Hat Guy give Jethro a message in code?"

"We won't know until we crack the code, dummy," Martinez said. "I'm going to crack it. Cryptology. That's my thing. It's my calling."

I'd never heard him say the word "cryptology" before, but okay.

"We can save Jethro like we saved Easy," he said. "I'll do the secret stuff. You do the legwork."

"If we're saving him like Easy, you mean life in prison instead of death," I said. And I thought of all those dogs that were going to be put down at the shelter. Guilt sat on me heavy as a hippo.

"Don't be a jerk," Martinez said. "Life and death, that's a big difference. And if we don't defend the defenseless, who will? Especially you. You're a world-famous lawyer now."

I sighed. But he was right. If no one else is doing the right thing, you have to stand up and be the one.

"Okay, we'll take the case," I said. "But we have to keep our work on the down-low. Now go to bed."

Slowly I drifted off to sleep again, but Ilia and Taleesa and Mario were gone. Instead, I dreamed about yellowed pages with squiggles and nonsense words, just waiting to be decoded.

7

To be honest, for the next week, I was too busy to even think about Jethro Gersham. Martinez was working on his codes. And I had a bunch of "Pet of the Week" profiles to write for the Houmahatchee *Herald*.

It was weird how the *Herald* column worked out. Miss Megg gave me the name and number of an editor to call about bringing the column back to life. Taleesa said it would be better to go in person and talk to someone.

"It's always better to work for an editor who's seen your face," she said. "It's not far. You should be able to take your bike."

The newspaper office wasn't what I expected. Even though I knew the Houmahatchee *Herald* was printed right here in town, I'd always imagined they worked in a tall building with rows and rows of desks on an open floor as big as Walmart. There would be phones that rang all the time and printers that made click-clacking sounds and some old guy mixing cocktails at his desk and a mean old editor who comes out of his office and shouts, "Peale, GET IN HERE!!" An awesome, cool madhouse.

When I pulled up to the *Herald* I realized I'd passed the building a thousand times. It was in an old Burger Meister restaurant that closed before I was born. When I was little, you could still see the Burger Meister sign that someone had torn down and thrown out back. Now the sign was covered in kudzu. Only now did I notice the little black-and-white "Houmahatchee Herald" sign over the door, in that old-timey newspaper writing that nobody can read.

A bell on the door dinged when I went in. There was nobody there. It still looked a lot like a Burger Meister. The counter was still there, but behind it, in the kitchen, there were filing cabinets and a bunch of bright studio lights on stands, like photographers use. There was still brown-and-orange tile on the floor, like at a Burger Meister, and all the yellow-topped Burger Meister tables were still there, only now they were piled with newspapers and boxes of paper and a couple of computers. In the corner, where the drink stand would normally be, there was a bulletproof vest sort of slumped against the wall, with a military helmet propped on top of it as if the Martians had vaporized a soldier right there. Next to that stood a five-foot statue of Meisterburger, the Burger Meister mascot, only instead of holding out a big plaster burger on a tray, he held a tray stacked with wooden plaques.

"I'll be right there," shouted a voice from what, at a Burger Meister, would have been a bathroom.

I'm a snoop, so I picked up the plaques on Meisterburger's tray. They were all awards, for "investigative reporting" and "deadline reporting."

I heard a flush and then out came a white guy who looked

a little younger than Dad, blond but already losing a lot of hair on top and wearing a button-up shirt with a ketchup stain on the front.

"Sorry about that," he said, extending a hand. "Ricky Braxton. Ricky with a Y."

"Atticus Peale," I said. "I'd like a Meister Burger, large, with fries please."

He laughed. "Wouldn't we all? You're here for the Pet-of-the-Week thing, right?"

"That's right," I said. "I didn't realize this building was the newspaper. I thought it was a place where druggies sleep at night."

"Nope," Braxton said. "We fired that guy."

I dug into my backpack. "I've got a résumé here. And Taleesa, my stepmom, said I should bring writing samples, so here's a fantasy novella I wr—"

"You're hired," he said. "Not that it's a paying job. But you've got it."

He headed back toward the tables with computers and motioned me to come along.

"That's it?" I said. "I mean, you'll just let a twelve-year-old write a column in your paper without an interview?"

"We're a very small operation," he said. "I'm the editor. My wife, Rickie with an I-E, is the only writer and the only photographer. If you read the paper regularly—I'm sure that's what preteen girls just love to do—you'll see that the entire front page is written by Rickie Braxton or Ricky Braxton. On the inside, world news from the Associated Press and then community news, written by the community." He handed me a newspaper. "Just look. Here's notes from the Daughters of the Confederacy meeting. A weekly column by a local preacher. Another column by the mayor, who never meets his deadline. All of them have to have a ton of edits before we can put them in print. What I really, desperately need is photos, photos of something other than the Daughters giving medals to old guys again and again. People love animal stories."

"How many do you need per week?" I asked.

"As many as you can write," he said. He squinted at the seventy-page manuscript in my hand. "I take it back. Four. No more than two hundred words each. The trick is making each one of them fresh when you're writing the same thing again and again. Have them to us by 5 p.m. every Wednesday."

"Do I get a—what do you call it—where you have your name at top of the story?"

"A byline? Do you want a byline?"

I thought about the trouble I'd already gotten into with the *Daily Royal Post*. "I'd rather not."

"Then you can't have one. Any questions?"

"Yeah," I said. "What're the helmet and vest for?"

"To stop bullets," he said. "They don't really work. Turns out you have to know someone's shooting at you beforehand, so you can put them on. Not as useful as you might think."

He saw the shocked look on my face.

"We sent a reporter to Iraq, with the National Guard, a long time ago," he said. "In better times, when the newspaper had more money."

And that was it. I was a newspaper columnist. After a day of cleaning dog poop, washing dogs, and walking dogs, I'd sit at the table with dog pictures and my phone and I'd thumb-type little riffs about dogs and cats. It was hard, like writing poetry.

```
HANS AND FRANZ

These kitten brothers do everything
together. Cuddle, chase bugs, play with
yarn. They almost suffocated together,
when someone dropped them off in a
stapled-up paper bag. They could find a
home together too. Will it be yours?
```

"The paper bag thing is a little edgy," said Taleesa, looking over from her own writing. "But maybe it will grab some-body's attention."

```
JOY
This happy mutt is aptly named. She's
```

"Happy is too plain," I said. "Taleesa, what's a better word for happy?"

"Joyful," she said.

"The dog's already named Joy."

"Change the name. Joy is a fairly common name. People might ignore it. What if you just rename the dog Joyful?"

"I can do that?" I said. "Okay. Joyful it is."

My phone double-beeped. A text message.

Princess_P: YOU THINK YOUR SO COOL BEING A DOG LAWYER BUT YOUR GOING TO JAIL

Ugh. Who was Princess P? Some girl from school, no doubt. I'm not super-popular, but I didn't know of anybody who hated me. Strange.

atticustpeale: Learn punctuation.

I went back to writing, but it bothered me. Jail. Was that a real possibility after all?

Princess_P: EVEN IF YOU DON'T GET JAIL, YOUR LIFE WILL FEEL LIKE JAIL WHEN SCHOOL STARTS. NOBODY LIKES YOU.

atticustpeale: GO JUMP IN THE LAKE, MARTINEZ. THIS IS NOT FUNNY.

Princess_P: I'M NOT YOUR MONKEY BROTHER. WHAT IS WRONG WITH YOU'RE FAMILY? YOU DEFEND KILLERS, YOU SHOULD BE ASHAMED.

"What's wrong, Atty?" Taleesa said. "You look like you saw a ghost."

"It's nothing, I'm cool," I said. Well, Princess P definitely wasn't Martinez. Who uses slurs like that, really? I tried to think of a girl at school who would stoop that low.

Another double-beep.

Princess_P: JUST LOOK AT THE COMMENTS OF THE ROYAL POST STORY. YOU DESERVE IT.

I went back to the *Royal Post* column. In the comments was this:

> **Attythedoglawyer:** I'm Atticus T. Peale. Me and my monkey brother defend dogs that bite. My dad defends murderers. Someone should come to our house at 922 Burnt Corn Creek Road, Houmahatchee Alabama and give us what we deserve.

I pushed away from the table.

"You're right, Taleesa," I said. "I don't feel so good. I'm going to lie down in my room and play with McNutters."

Even McNutters, in his hot tub with his martini, wasn't safe. Every knock on the dollhouse door made him wet himself in fear.

Half an hour later, I looked at the *Royal Post* story again.

> **Attythedoglawyer:** <THIS COMMENTER HAS BEEN BLOCKED FOR VIOLATING THE ROYAL POST'S SOCIAL MEDIA POLICIES>

The door creaked open. It was Martinez.

"Are you okay, Atty?" He looked like he did as a baby, when he'd ask me to pick him up. "Dad worries all the time. But when you or Mom look worried, I get worried."

I took a deep breath. "I'm totally fine, dude. Get out of here. McNutters is naked."

My brother, at 922 Burnt Corn Creek Road. Just another troll on the Internet, I told myself. But I also thought about that Army helmet and vest at the *Herald. Turns out you have to know beforehand that someone is shooting at you . . .*

8

I don't know how it is for you, but in my world, grown-ups are always whining about how we kids don't play outside enough. What is out there, really, to play with? All the computers and pens and paper and easels and paints are inside. I'm already outside the dollhouse, isn't that enough?

And when there *is* cool stuff to do out there, it's not the kind of stuff our parents would let us do. Dad and Taleesa have these fond childhood memories of stealing shopping carts, rooting around in dumpsters, shooting water moccasins with a shotgun, and barfing after accidentally swallowing chewing tobacco. Like they'd really let us do any of that!

Luckily for Martinez and me, there was always a way out of this playing-outside madness. It had a lot to do with alligators. And a lot to do with the fact that we're on the Alabama side of the state line.

Twenty miles south of here, in Florida, gators are as

common as possums, and are viewed pretty much the same way. Kids in kindergarten get alligator-safety coloring books. ("Never feed an alligator. Don't swim in swamps. Keep your little dog on a leash.") Florida people are proud of that. They're proud that they know enough to avoid gators—and that they know enough not to freak out every time they look out into the water and see little eyes looking back. "Of course you saw a big gator crawl up out of the water," Florida folks will say. "It's sunset. That's what gators do."

It's different here. Sure, we don't have as many big reptiles lying around. But the big thing is that we see gators the way the rest of the non-Florida world sees them. An alligator is a mascot, a zoo animal. It's like having a tiger in your kiddie pool or finding a dragon on the creek bank.

Strudwick County, in particular, has its own very specific gator legend. In Dead Beaver Swamp, an algae-choked lake north of Houmahatchee, a twenty-foot gator lurked in the water. Or so rumor had it. If you've ever seen an alligator, you know they're sort of like bug-eyed goldfish; the longer they live and the bigger they get, the more strange and bumpy they look. So the Swamp Monster, as some people called it, was a knobby-backed gray-and-black behemoth with fat muscular Jabba arms and brilliant white teeth the size of your fingers.

Everybody saw the Swamp Monster and nobody saw the Swamp Monster. There were no photos of the thing, yet every time a four-foot gator crawled out of a drainpipe, people would call the cops and report a monster sighting. Once when a little three-footer settled in beside the loading docks for the school cafeteria, they put the whole school on lockdown. Small gators were a sign that the Swamp Monster was near, I guess. Even though he was a male gator in almost all the stories, the Swamp Monster was like a queen bee, churning out thousands of gator eggs in the swamp every night.

A dumb story, but it worked when kids really needed it. If you ever needed a scary tale to tell around the campfire, the Swamp Monster always worked because you could convince people it was real: it happened to a kid I knew who went to Snoad Middle, and now he doesn't have any legs.

And even smart parents like mine would let you stay inside if you told them thought you saw a gator in the bushes. So I guess I'm a spreader of the legend, too. I've never been afraid to mention my gator-fear on hot summer days when Taleesa wants us out of the house so she can write.

I never thought I'd see the Swamp Monster in real life, much less become its lawyer. But life has a way of swimming up and biting you when you least expect it.

It happened one morning when Taleesa was driving us to the animal shelter. I always get the front seat because I'm bigger, and before I started working at the animal shelter, I'd look out the window and watch the landscape roll by. The trailers, the rows of slash pine, then Dead Beaver Swamp, where, if you were lucky, you might see a crane wading around in the shallows.

But not anymore. After I started writing the column for the *Herald*, I spent every moment texting. Texting in the car, on the toilet, at the breakfast table.

HERALD_EDITOR: There are some missing words in Joyful's profile. I marked them in Google Docs if you have a minute.

MEGG: I'm speaking at the County Commission this morning. Please work the front desk until I return.

Princess_P: Your a frak. Your mother was a freak. You don't belong here.

Princess_P: Freak.

404-555-5515: We are in Atlanta. If we come down Wednesday to adopt Frida, can we meet Atty the Dog Lawyer?

Atticustpeale: You're talking to her. We can't hold any dog if someone else shows up to adopt first, but I'll be here.

The car pulled to a stop, and I pocketed my phone. But when I looked up, we weren't at the shelter. We were on the side of the road, on the banks of Dead Beaver Swamp. A bunch of SUVs with flashing police lights were parked along the bank, and some big, burly guys were backing a flat boat into the water. A bit further up the road, a little aluminum boat lay up on the bank, with mud—and what looked like blood—spattered all over the front. Yuck.

Taleesa unhitched her seat belt. "I get the feeling there's a story here."

I snorted. "What? You're going to just go up and pester the cops while they're working?"

"I'm a journalist," Taleesa said. "It's very empowering." She flipped through her pocketbook, looking at business cards for all the magazines she's written for. "*Black Belt Outdoors*," she said, pulling one out. "Freelance correspondent. I'll be back in a minute."

"I'm coming," I said.

"Nuh-uh," Taleesa said, putting on a surprisingly good white-guy twang. "You'll git eat by the Swump Munster."

"Gators only eat small children," I said. "I'm twelve. I'm plenty big."

("Fat ugly girl," Princess P had said. "No boy wants a 12-year-old with a muffin top.")

"Okay, you come," Taleesa said. "But you stay with me. And Martinez, you stay in the car."

Martinez fluttered his eyelashes at me, trilled in a girl voice: "Tell Troy Butler I said hi."

"Shut up," I said. "I love you, but sometimes I hate you."

As it turns out, Butler actually was there, with mud up to the knees of his uniform and a slash of blood across his shirt. He was typing on a laptop propped on the hood of an SUV. He smiled when he saw us.

"Miss Peale," he said, nodding. "And this must be . . ."

"Miz Peale, the elder," Taleesa said. "If it's not too much of a hassle, we were just driving by and wondered what's going on."

Butler sighed. "There was a monster of *some* sort in the lake last night. Bunch of guys were out hunting, had too many beers, and decided they'd get famous by capturing the

Swamp Monster on video. They went out on a boat with flashlights and cell phones, and one of them saw some eyes shining back. Pointed his phone right at those eyes. Well, he doesn't have that phone anymore. Or his hand."

"The Monster got him," I said. "So the Monster is real."

"Well, a gator got him," Butler said. "Guy's lucky to be alive. His drunk friends did an okay job of getting him back in the boat, tying off the arm, and all that. I just happened to be driving by to work, and they flagged me down. Who's the monster here, and who's just going about their business, I guess it depends on how you look at it. At any rate, these guys"—he hooked his thumb back at the guys putting their boat in the water—"are going to troll the lake for the gator and kill it."

Taleesa looked at me. "A hunt for the Swamp Monster. Now that's a story."

"I'm pretty sure that's illegal," I said. "Alligator-hunting season doesn't start until August. It's against the law to kill gator out of season. It's in Title Nine of the state code." They both looked at me like I'd grown an extra head. "Hunting laws, y'all. I was curious, so I read them all."

Butler shook his head. "This isn't normal alligator hunting. The state has the power to declare a gator a nuisance alligator. That means it's a danger to humans. And then it can be killed."

I looked out at the mists on Dead Beaver Swamp. They called it that because, years ago, somebody wanted to drain it, and they thought all they needed to do was knock down a beaver dam on Clay Creek not far from here. So they went in and slaughtered all the beavers and blew up the dam, but the swamp stayed swampy.

"I don't understand how an alligator in a swamp is a nuisance," I said. "If an alligator's in my house, that's a nuisance and a danger. That guy was in the alligator's house."

"You'll have to take it up with the state Department of Conservation," Butler said. "And about that other thing—"

"Oh, I'll take it up with the department," I said, cutting him off on purpose. "Believe me, I will."

Before my life got filled up with dogs and deputies and alligators, one of my major goals in life was trying to find a way to avoid seventh grade. I've researched seventh grade quite thoroughly and I'm sure no good can come of it.

"Girls enter the middle school years as confident children and often leave as broken, anxiety ridden young women obsessed with pleasing everyone," writes Rachel McMartin, PhD, author of the book *Saving Emmeline Grangerford: A Study in Teen Mopiness Among Girls*.

"All the key pathologies of manhood—avoidance of responsibility, anger toward women, obsession with violence—are picked up by boys in early adolescence," writes Dr. K.V. S. Singh in *Hamlet Was Fat: Rescuing Boys from Computer Culture*.

I've clipped and copied dozens of these quotes. Grown-ups have written, like, a thousand books about how awful sixth and seventh and eighth grades are. They talk about this time in their life like it was a war they barely survived. Yet they're the ones who keep pushing us into this weird stuff. We've organized a school dance, who are you going to bring? No more kickball—now football is for boys and cheerleading is for girls. Here's a test to determine your career interests. There's no way to fail, they say.

(There is in fact a way to fail the career interest test. Write "I WANT TO BE QUEEN OF NABOO" on the top of each page. That will land you in the office.)

My solution: cancel the whole middle school/junior high thing. Send everybody home for three years with a reading list. We all return as confident people with deep voices and bras and learner's permits and we go on with our lives. Before I met Easy, my plan for the summer was to write out a long argument for why I should homeschool the next year.

But reminders of school kept popping up. "I haven't heard you practice your flute all summer," Taleesa said more than once. Three or four times, when I opened my lunch box at the animal shelter, I found a paperback copy of *Far Huntress*, a book about a girl in a dark future who has to become an assassin for an evil dictator in order to save her professor father from being executed. It's our summer reading. Sounds like a good book, actually, but I just wasn't ready to think about school.

Which is why I was so disappointed to see Peyton Vebelstadt at the animal shelter when we got there. I was late, I had swamp mud on my shoes, and now I have to see a classmate.

It's not that I don't like Peyton. I guess I have a tiny crush on her. She's so tall, the tallest person in our class, and she has this long, long reddish hair that always looks so soft. And here's the thing: she never *talks* about her hair the way other long-haired girls do. Teachers used to accuse her of wearing eye makeup because she has these big round eyes that I, at least, think are really beautiful. When they make a movie of my life, I want Peyton to play the role of me.

("Fat ugly girl," Princess_P said in her text.)

And Peyton is, you know, nice. Not bland and sweet but just chummy with everybody. She never says anything snarky like I do all the time, and I've never seen her be mean to anybody. I can't tell you one thing about what's inside her head—does she secretly want to be a vampire or to run people over with a car?—but everybody who knows her thinks of her warmly. I'd like to be that kind of person, but I don't want it enough to actually do it.

So, yeah, I like Peyton. But I don't ever want to see school people in the summer. You know?

There she was, in the lobby of the animal shelter, cuddling a long-haired, pug-faced cat. I felt that lurch of school dread. Then Peyton turned and smiled at me, and I couldn't help but laugh. Pretty smiling girl, grim serious cat.

"That's Wednesday," I said. "Her brother's name is Pugsley. It would be great if you could take both of them."

"Oh, Atty, I know," Peyton said. "I saw you and Martinez with them on YouTube. They're so cute!"

Yes, Martinez got me to present both cats on his YouTube channel. He kept me mostly out of the frame, but you could still hear my voice with its weird twang.

"Take them home," I said to Peyton. "Both of them. You'd be a good cat mom."

"Oh, I will," she said. "That's what I came here for." She stood there staring into Wednesday's eyes, Peyton in her short shorts and her skinny legs that went on and on like a three-hour movie. It's not fair how some things, like being tall, are so easy for some people.

"You know," I said, "you should volunteer with us. You'd be great in those videos. I can tell you really love cats."

"Oh, Atty," she said. "I really admire what you do. Going to court, risking jail and all. But I don't think I could do it."

"What? Who says I'm risking jail?"

"Oh, I don't know, it was on the Internet or something," she said. "I'm just not—I can't do what you do. You know, girls at school are so mean. And boys, who knows what they're thinking? When you do something, don't you ever worry about what people will think?"

"I guess I don't," I said. "Why would a mean girl at school care what I do at the animal shelter? Why would a boy care? Have you heard something?"

Peyton looked at me like I was a kitten, still in the cage.

"Oh, Atty," she said. "Look, I just keep hearing that seventh grade is hard. There are girls at my church who are already plotting how they're going to become popular, and who's going to be their friend and who's not. It's scary. I think it's a good time to just keep your head down."

"Wait a minute," I said. "Princess P. You know who she is, don't you?"

"A character from a video game?"

"No, she's a girl who—oh never mind," I said. "Look, I guess I do care what people think, a little. I didn't used to, but I'm starting to. And you know what? So far it completely sucks, caring what people think. How can I control what someone else thinks? How am I supposed to not be a weirdo, in someone else's eyes? What are the rules for that? Heck, what do *you* think of me?"

"I think you're very brave," she said. "You're like that girl from Afghanistan. The one who got shot for going to school."

Wow. Me, like Malala Yousafzai. She was serious, I could see it in her eyes. How could I ever live up to that?

"But what's her life like?" Peyton continued. "I mean, can you imagine her going out with boys? Shopping? Just hanging around and being a girl? Don't you want that in life? Before you grow up?"

That Malala compliment made me feel pretty brave. "Maybe I don't," I said. "Maybe I don't have a choice. Maybe I have to do this."

"Well, everybody has a choice, Atty," Peyton said.

"I guess I've already made mine," I said. "I chose to get Wednesday and Pugsley a home, and now they have a home. How can I stop?"

And I decided right then and there. I'd write a legal brief as soon as I got home. A brief about alligators.

9

"It appears that we have young Miss Peale here again," Judge Grover said, peering down at my brief through his bifocals.

"Your Honor," I said, standing up straight.

It took us forever to find a simple black dress in my size, but now that I was before the judge, I was glad I wasn't wearing something frilly.

"And who's here for the state?"

Backsley Graddoch stood up beside me. "The attorney general has asked me to take up this little matter on his behalf," he said.

Grover grunted and stared down at my brief, flipping through the pages for an uncomfortably long time.

"For the sake of the audience," he said, "let me go over what Miss Peale is requesting. Miss Peale, you're asking me, a circuit court judge in Houmahatchee, to enjoin the governor of this state to rescind his order to find and kill a large alligator known popularly as the Swamp Monster."

"Objection, Your Honor," I said. "We don't know that the gator in question—or any real existing gator—is the same gator referred to in the 'Swamp Monster' legend."

"You can't object to what a judge says, young lady," Grover said. "Save that for your opponent."

Stand straight, I told myself. When you talk, talk loud and slow.

"My apologies, Your Honor," I said.

"Soooo . . . You're arguing from the state Administrative Code, Section 220-2-.95. Yet as I read it here, even as quoted in your brief, an alligator that has attacked people shall be regarded as a nuisance alligator. Am I right?"

"Yes, Your Honor."

"And the state may assess the situation and determine whether the alligator shall be killed or removed, am I correct?"

"Yes, Your Honor," I said. "The folks from the Conservation Department have been saying state law requires the alligator to be killed. But the code itself says the situation will be assessed, and a decision will be made either to kill the alligator or to move it from the swamp. There's no evidence that that assessment was ever done, or that the governor was even presented with the idea that he has a choice."

"But you're not arguing that the law blocks the governor from choosing to order an alligator hunt?" Grover asked.

"Your Honor, here's the context. A man provokes an alligator when he knows he shouldn't, and he gets bitten. Now there's a hunt in the swamp for an alligator—any alligator—to pay for that supposed crime. And alligators are still rare enough in Alabama that they're protected by law.

So there's a question, first of all, of whether this so-called attack is really an attack. If an alligator came up out of the water and bit an unsuspecting person, it's fair to say that is an attack. But if you go where the animal is and provoke it, is that an attack by the animal? I think not. Second, there's the issue of whether there's any serious effort being made to catch the right anim—"

"I'm going to cut you off right here, Miz Peale," Judge Grover said. "Are you a lawyer?"

"I am not," I said. "I'm representing myself. I've never said I'm a lawyer."

Well, not in public anyway. What I think of myself is my business. Isn't it?

"You're not representing or defending an alligator?"

"No, Your Honor," I said. "I'm arguing that as a citizen of this state, I have a right to see environmental laws in my county enforced. Including laws that protect the alligator population."

"So can you tell me this: how does your right to have an alligator in the local swamp outweigh the right of all other residents of this county to feel safe from a wild animal attack?"

Oh God, I'm blank! That question! It was like that time I fell down the stairs at school and had the wind knocked out of me.

Grover turned to Graddoch. "Does the state have anything to add?"

"The governor is the chief executive of Alabama, Your Honor," Graddoch said. "That's all."

Grover leaned back and threw down his bifocals. "This

is a frivolous pleading, Miss Peale, and I'm dismissing it. If I see you again, I hope you bring something worth this court's time. That's all."

Ever seen a movie about the high school prom? There's always some nerdy boy who asks a pretty girl to go with him. Down on his knee, in front of everybody. And she says no. And he has to accept forever that this person will never love him. And he has to stand, and turn. And walk down the hallway with all those people watching him.

I've learned that this happens to everybody, at some point. At least I was already standing. At least I didn't have a bunch of dumb flowers in my hand. I tried to hold my head up high as I walked down the aisle and out into the hallway, where the news cameras and the bright lights were waiting.

⚖️ ⚖️ ⚖️

Bing.

> **CinqueMartinez:** Check out this story. They call you "defender of monsters." Cool.

This at nearly midnight, while I'm lying in bed, trying to sleep. I can't sleep. What just happened?
Bing.

> **Princess_P:** Personally I think you'd look great with one hand bitten off.

And with that message, a link to a video of Raybun G. Hardstetter, the guy who was bitten by the alligator. A local TV station had interviewed him in his hospital room.

"A local man—attacked by the alligator some call the Swamp Monster—says faith in God helped him survive against the odds," the reporter said. Then the scene shifted to the hospital bed. Raybun in a hospital gown, talking about how he felt his arm snap and immediately called on Jesus to help him make it back to the surface.

"I feel like the Devil himself had a holt of me," he said. "I know I wasn't living right. Drinking and chasing women and staying up all night. That's how I wound up out there hunting for the Devil himself. I always believed in Jesus. But if you're not really following Him, you're just out there searching in the dark like me.

"Sin is like that," he continued. "First you're ignoring the risk and having fun. Then Satan gets a holt of you with teeth, the strongest teeth you ever felt. And he drags you down into the dark, spinning you around. And that's when I said to Jesus, if he would let me live, I'd do right. And just then my hand tore away and I swam off fast as I could. Just like in the Bible, if your hand offends you, cut it off."

Then the reporter asks him what he thinks of the "devil's advocate" who was petitioning to save the gator.

"I don't know what would make a little girl do such a thing," Raybun said, looking into the camera. "But I know that if she'd let Jesus into her heart, she wouldn't need all this attention."

I groaned. So many emotions, so little time. Of course I felt sorry for the guy. The way he admitted he shouldn't have been there, the way he called on Jesus, all very moving. And yet, my client—well, the animal I'm helping—is the Devil in this story. And I'm a sinner. How is this story about Jesus and my heart? He was saying that my life of cleaning dog poop was just like his pre-gator life of drinking and dancing and hunting deer with a spotlight. It's all non-Jesus stuff you shouldn't be doing.

Anger. That's what I was feeling, I decided. That way leads to the dark side. And it keeps you awake, when you have videos to make and cat profiles to write and cages to clean in the morning.

Bing.

CinqueMartinez: I've broken the code.

Atticustpeale: What code?

CinqueMartinez: The code on that piece of paper. The one stapled to the lottery ticket in Dad's case.

Atticustpeale: Sneak over and talk to me in person.

A couple minutes later my door creaked open. In the moonlight, I saw Martinez in his too-short pajamas. If you demand PJs with dinosaurs on them, at some point you have to accept pajamas that are too short. Martinez climbed right into bed with me, like he did when we were little and shared a room.

"I've got it, Atty," he said. "After long expert study, I've figured it out. It's complete nonsense."

"Umm, if it's nonsense then you haven't broken any code," I said.

"No, look," he said, holding up his phone, with the photo of the paper on it. "Look at the pattern of letters."

wefpoj
wf;l
qpweodfk
pfoj
'sdlfkef

"Okayyyy," I said.

"Now look at your own phone. The keyboard," he said. "There, you see it?"

I looked from one phone to the other. "Martinez, is this some kind of face-on-Mars conspiracy thing?"

"No, look at where the letters are on the keyboard." he said. "W-E-F on one side. P-O-L and J on the other."

"So a cat walked on a keyboard," I said. "He stepped here and here. What does it prove?"

"A cat. Or somebody just banged their hands here and here and purposely typed out nonsense. A keyboard smash."

"So what?"

"So, when the police capture Jethro he has this little slip of paper stapled to the lottery ticket. Why on earth would somebody staple that to the lottery ticket?"

I just sighed. Martinez shook his head like I was being really stupid.

"Look," he said. "Do we know if Jethro can read? What if he can't? And what's it like going to the store if you can't read?"

I'd never thought about it before. "I guess you can't use a debit card machine if you can't read. You'd have to pay for stuff with cash, I guess."

"And then when you're done they hand you a . . ."

"A receipt!" I said. "Okay, I get you now. You're saying *this* is the receipt Jethro talked about getting from the clerk. Somebody goes to a typewriter and types out a nonsense page. Then they staple it to the lottery ticket. Then they say, 'here's your receipt,' and he takes both. He doesn't even know he's got a lottery ticket."

"Code broken," Martinez said.

"I don't know if that's really codebreaking," I said. "But it's big. If you're right, that's big."

"You're just jealous." Martinez said. "I'm a codebreaker."

"Well, we have to tell Dad, obviously."

"I'm not telling him. I wasn't supposed to take the picture of the paper. Why don't we just write him an anonymous note?"

"Like he wouldn't know immediately who wrote it."

"You tell him," Martinez said. "You're the dog lawyer. You're good at speaking for people. Go be my lawyer."

I glanced at the phone again. 1:13 a.m. There was a little strip of light under my door, so either Martinez left a light on or one of the parents was still up, reading and typing.

"OK, Martinez," I said. "You go back to bed."

"I'm comfy right here. I'll just snooze a bit while you go."

Little brothers. I climbed over Martinez and headed for the door.

Walking around our house at night, I often feel like I'm on some old wooden ship in the British Navy. Our house turned one hundred years old that summer; it isn't some big plantation house like you see in travel brochures, just a normal-sized house, but it is plenty creaky. The floorboards wobble, the hallway closet door pops open every time you walk by. You can't sneak up on anybody.

But Dad didn't seem to notice me. He was on the couch, still in his suit, with papers all around and a computer on his lap.

"Hey," I said. "The murder case."

Dad nodded. "You know, in law school, I decided I'd defend poor clients because it would help me to sleep at night. And here I am. If I were a tax lawyer, I'd be in bed right now."

"I'm having the same problem," I said. "People keep texting me about the alligator case."

"Let me guess," he said. "You're on the side of monsters. You're what's wrong with this country. If you'd worked a day in your life, you'd have enough principles not to defend a killer."

"Are you reading my emails?" I asked. I was serious, though it didn't sound like something he'd do.

"I don't have to," he said. "Look, I guess I should have told you before. This is the price of the kind of work we do. People say mean things. You stay up at night. You think there's just one case out there that needs your help and then you find there's more work than you can ever, ever finish."

I moved some papers and sat beside him. A long silence.

"And?" I said. "This is where you're supposed to say something inspiring about why we do what we do. About how important it is to stand up for the defenseless, even if you know you can't win."

He laughed. "Do I really have to say it? I don't know another way to live. Looks like you don't, either."

"I'm sure there's another way to live. You could drink all day and fall asleep in the hot tub like McNutters."

"Sounds dangerous."

Silence.

"Dad, I've got something to tell you, but I want you to promise not to be mad," I said.

"I can't make promises about emotions," he said. "I promise I'll be less angry because you told me yourself."

And I told him all about Martinez and the photo and the code.

"Wow," he said. "Wow, that is big indeed. Why didn't I think of that? So somebody could have given Jethro the lottery ticket and made him think it was just a receipt. But who?"

"Didn't the owner of the pawnshop have a business partner?" I asked.

"He has an alibi," Dad said. "Fishing all day. He has a receipt from the marina where he put his boat in. Still, if it's true Jethro can't read, it supports his side of the story. I hope I get a chance to use that in court. I hope."

"When is the trial, anyway?" I asked.

"I don't know," Dad said. "Maybe there won't be one."

"What?"

"Atty, you know I'm not supposed to talk about what goes on between me and my client," he said. "But you know, a lot of people plead guilty to things they know they didn't do, to get a lesser sentence. Especially when they could get the death penalty."

"So Jethro's going to plead," I said, shocked. Only then did I realize how convinced I was that he was innocent. "I just don't see how he can do that when he knows he didn't do it."

"That kind of thing is less about guilt or innocence than it is about your faith in the system, I guess. Or your faith in your lawyer. Do you think you can win? Put yourself in the shoes of a person accused of a crime and you'll see what I mean."

I looked down at my feet, I guess because of the "shoes" comment.

"Dad," I said. "I have something else to tell you. I have in fact been accused of a crime."

"Practicing law without a license," Dad said, matter-of-factly.

"You knew!"

"Troy Butler came to see me. I shut him down pretty good. You've got nothing to worry about, but I was wondering when you were going to tell me."

"Maybe I wanted to fight my own battles," I said. But I knew it was wrong, even as I was saying it. "Dad, do you ever feel like it's easy to speak for other people, but really hard to speak for yourself? Easy to take care of other people, but hard to take care of yourself?"

"Story of my life," he said. "Speaking of which, you should go get some sleep."

"Can I borrow your computer first? I want to write a letter to the governor about the alligator."

"It's one-thirty! I'll give you fifteen minutes. Look up his official e-mail address. Write a *short* e-mail, proof it, then send. Fifteen minutes. Then bed."

By the time I hit "send," Dad was snoring next to me on the couch. I leaned against him and closed my eyes. It felt good to know I wasn't in trouble with him. All that guilt about the lawyer-without-a-license charge, for nothing.

Next thing I knew, it was daylight. Martinez standing about a foot from the TV, in his PJs, eating Froot Loops. My phone was jangling in my hand. I picked it up.

"H'lo?" I said.

"Hi, can I speak to Atticus Peale, or one of his parents?"

"This is she."

"This is Jen Carter, a spokeswoman for Governor Fischer King. We got your message, and the governor would like to meet you to talk about your letter."

I jumped up and did a little dance. Dad's laptop clattered to the floor.

"Just name a time," I said.

10

T here's a bullet hole in our living room. A dent, really, on the mantel just to the left of where Martinez hangs his stocking at Christmas. I know it was made by a bullet, because I was standing right there when the bullet came in.

This happened years ago. It was, for us, a normal Saturday evening. Martinez was sitting on the floor next to the coffee table, which he'd covered from edge to edge with Lego buildings. Now two Lego men were fighting over who would be king of the city, and Martinez was speaking the entire drama out loud. "Aaaaah! Take that, you traitor!" he said. Taleesa was ironing in the kitchen, and she was talking to herself, too. She always talks out the dialogue in her fiction, and I've learned not to be alarmed when she mumbles to herself about why she sold secrets to Russia, or why she spent fifteen years working on a fishing boat. Dad, meanwhile, was in his study talking to the walls about "my client." He had a trial coming up and he always practiced his closing arguments that way. Sometimes I think I'm the only person in the house who doesn't talk to herself constantly. But then, here I am, talking to you.

I was eight years old when this happened, and I'd just written my first novel. It was about fifteen pages long and was about a girl stranded on a desert island. At the time I wrote it, I thought a desert island was actual desert—sand and no water—and when I found out it just meant "deserted," I was embarrassed and resolved to burn the novel so no one would ever find it.

So there I was, standing in the living room by the fireplace, when suddenly there was all this commotion outside. A loud pickup roared by on the street, the driver honking his horn again and again. Somebody down the street shouted some kind of war whoop.

And then the gunshots. Pop. Pop. Pop pop pop pop pop. A second later, a tinkle of broken glass, a strange, sudden click from the fireplace, and something thumped me on the chest and bounced away.

I'm sure you've heard of Iron Bowl, the big football game between Alabama and Auburn. People are obsessed with it, and when the game ends, folks who supported the winning team drive around and shout and sometimes shoot guns into the air. Pop pop pop pop pop. All bullets have to come down somewhere. And one of them came through our living room window, knocked a chip of wood out of the mantel, and bounced off. The cops later found both the wood chip and the bullet on the living room floor. They say the bullet had already lost a lot of its speed, which is why it didn't go all the way into the wood. The cops said it was the wood chip that thumped me in the chest, but I think it was the bullet itself.

I brought all that up to say this. There are a lot of things that other Alabamians do that I've never done. Every other family in the state was watching the Iron Bowl that Saturday. No one in my house even thought about it until the gunshots started popping off. Dad and Taleesa are the only grown-ups I know who don't care about football. I'm the only white girl I know who's never watched *Gone with the Wind*. And I'm the only kid I know who's never been baptized or bat mitzvahed into any religion whatsoever. (Martinez got christened as a baby, because Old Martinez, Taleesa's dad, demanded it.)

Even when I want to do the typical Alabama thing, fate seems to stop me. Every year, fourth-graders from across Alabama make the journey to Montgomery as part of their Alabama history classes. You can see the capitol and Martin Luther King's house and the place where Nat King Cole was born and the White House of the Confederacy and a museum with a bus just like the one Rosa Parks sat in. Or so I am told. Dad says about half the photos in my Alabama history book were shot within six blocks of the capitol.

It's the one Alabama rite of passage I really wanted to experience, but I got the flu the day of the trip. So here I was, twelve years old already, and I'd never seen the capitol. I was extra-hyped about getting to see it now, with an invitation from the governor himself.

Taleesa took me to meet Gov. King, and she lost a free-lance job because of it. She was supposed to cover a bicycle race in Anniston for a sports magazine, but somebody had to drive me to Montgomery, and with Dad working a death penalty case, his job came first.

I know Taleesa was mad, because she was in comic book mode. Taleesa has never sold a comic book script, or even completed one, but when she's frustrated with Dad she starts coming up with ideas about superheroes and their screwed-up families.

"So there's a family with two moms," she said as we turned off the interstate. "Or at least, it *seems* like there are two moms. One is a superhero and the other one is a normal. But here's the thing: nobody, even the kids, ever sees the two moms in the same place at the same time. If Super Mom is taking care of the kids, Normal Mom is at the dentist. And when Normal Mom gets back, Super Mom just flies off to save the world. It's like Clark Kent and Superman. They haven't been in the same room for years. Are they the same person? Are they complete strangers, hired by some secret government agency to guard these super-kids? Do they even have a real relationship? And the biggest question: why does Normal Mom have to do so much of the work?"

Hey, I'll play along.

"So," I said. "What if Normal Mom is actually a super, too, but the agency decided her powers aren't as good as the other mom's, so they make her stay home with the kids?"

"Thank you," Taleesa said. "That's exactly what I'm talking about. We need to write this down."

And then we turned onto Dexter Avenue, the main street of downtown Montgomery. It was breathtaking, at least to me. Down at one end of the street, there was a fountain and a bunch of empty three-and four-story buildings, like some city street in a cop show. But you look up the street and there's the capitol building, big and gleaming white like a moon too close to earth.

"Oh man," Martinez said. "It looks just like the capitol in that movie, *Selma*."

"It *is* the capitol in the *Selma* movie," Taleesa said. "The same building. Martin Luther King stood right there and gave the speech. And look over to your right. That's Dexter Avenue Church, where Dr. King preached."

We came to a stoplight. I turned and, like, twenty feet away was a little brick church.

"Whaat?" I said. "Martin Luther King's church this close to the capitol? Good Lord, you could just about throw a rock from here and hit the capitol."

"You'd have to have a really good arm," Taleesa said.

"I could do it," Martinez said. "I could stand right there at Martin Luther King's church and throw a rock right through the capitol window and hit George Wallace right in the head."

Sigh. Little brothers.

"Let's set up a ground rule now," Taleesa said. "No talk about hitting any governor of Alabama in the head while we're in the governor's office. Promise me you won't say anything, Martinez, unless you're spoken to."

We parked right at the foot of the capitol steps, white steps that seemed to pour down the hillside like a waterfall. From the bottom of those steps you look up and you realize that the capitol is really, really big, like the giant's house at the top of the beanstalk.

"I'm just a bill, yes I'm only a bill," Martinez sang as we climbed the steps.

A giant's house. There were massive white columns, and on top of them a clock in a cube-shaped box. It looks like a normal wall clock at first, but as you approach, you realize that the clock is probably six feet tall. The capitol is a three-story building , with windows, but as you walk up you see that they're giant's windows, maybe fifteen feet tall. We walked past a statue of Jefferson Davis, glaring down at us and wearing a ridiculous cape. And there was a statue of some old-fashioned doctor in a lab coat that buttoned on the side.

"Cool," Martinez said. "They have statutes of Dracula and Dr. Frankenstein. I gotta get a picture of this!"

We walked right between the white columns to the front door—a big wooden door tall as a basketball hoop. From here, the capitol seemed to hang over us like a massive cliff.

"I can't do it," I said, stopping. "I forgot what I'm going to say. I had a whole speech ready and now I'm blank."

Taleesa put her hand on my shoulder. "Don't let it intimidate you," she said. "This door is big so you'll be afraid to knock. Remember, this whole thing was built during slavery times. It was built as a palace that neither you nor I were supposed to set foot in, except as servants. But it's our palace now. You just have to knock."

I reached out and knocked. Because Taleesa was watching, I knocked hard.

A hollow sound. No answer.

"Just open it," Taleesa said.

I turned the knob and we went in. Inside, there was a big quiet room that smelled like floor wax and soap. A swirly staircase to one side, that looked like a princess should come down it. And a green and brown metal desk where an old white cop with a crew cut sat. He stood and smiled.

"People always knock," he said. He was supposed to run us through a metal detector, but when we introduced ourselves, he waved us on.

"The governor's expecting you," he said. "Up the steps, turn left at the statue, and wait at the big doors."

At the top of the steps, a round room with a statue of a lady with big hair. Lurleen Wallace, the first woman governor. I know because it said so on a plaque. We turned left, down a hallway with big portraits of guys in old-fashioned clothes in creepy dark rooms. Taleesa said they were past governors, but I think they had a loose definition of what it means to be a governor, one that went all the way back to French and Spanish times. A couple of the paintings were of guys wearing lace and armor and long, curly hair like 1980s rock stars.

"Bigwigs," I said under my breath, just now understanding what that word meant.

"Dude, this is a full-on *castle*," Martinez said. "When I'm governor, I'll get my picture made with a fuzzy Russian hat, and a big sword, and a tiger sitting at my feet. Or maybe a wild pig, what do you call those?"

"A boar?" I said.

"No, no," Martinez said. "There's some other name. Dang. I can't think of it."

More big doors. Another cop, who nodded, picked up a radio and said: "The next appointment is here."

I looked around. The ceiling was so tall, the wood of the staircase nearby was so shiny. Martinez was right that this was a castle of sorts. Fifty years older than our historic house, without all the creaking and mouse holes and carroty smells and darkness. If you lived here, you could start thinking of yourself as some kind of princess. A bigwig.

The door opened, and another cop led us down another giant hall, to an office.

And there he was, standing by his secretary's desk. In white shirt and tie, without a coat, eating an Oreo and laughing with some guy in a suit. The governor of Alabama, Fischer King.

"Oh, hey," King said, chucking the cookie in the garbage and dusting off his hands. He was tall, older than Dad, handsome in a dull kind of way. He was clearly losing some of his hair, but the brown hair he did have was poofed up in a way that must have taken a lot of time with a hairdryer.

He stuck his hand out. "You must be Miz Peale."

I shook his hand, and, against my better judgment, kind of curtseyed a little. But after looking into his eyes I didn't feel nervous at all. He had a way of looking at you as though you were a long-lost friend.

"Oh," I said, grabbing Taleesa's hand. "And this is my mom."

The warm smile stayed, but King was at a loss for words for a second. He stuck out his hand at her. "Fischer King," he said.

"Taleesa Peale," she replied. "The evil stepmother."

"Ah, I see," he said. "Well you can't be all that evil to drive the kids all the way up from Houmahatchee on a workday. Your husband should be thankful."

A big grin from Taleesa. "You know, you're exactly right."

I pushed Martinez forward a little. "And this is my little brother," I said.

"Fischer King," the governor said.

Martinez took his hand and shook it.

"A peccary!" he said. "That's the kind of pig I was thinking of. When I'm governor, and they make my picture, if I can't have a pet tiger I'll have a peccary."

Taleesa buried her face in her hands. "He's a little too excited, Governor," she said. "We're going to the Montgomery Zoo after this, and . . ."

"Whoa!" Martinez said. "We're going to the zoo?"

King clapped Martinez on the shoulder. "We've got a great zoo, my friend."

"Do they have a peccary?" Martinez said.

Me: "Stop it, Martinez. Nobody knows what a peccary is."

"Oh, I know what a peccary is," King said. "A nocturnal gregarious wild swine. And they do have one. Y'all want to come into my office?"

He led us into a little hallway with a giant wooden emblem—the Great Seal of Alabama—hanging on one wall.

"That thing's way too big, idnit?" King said to me. "It's here for when guests come and want to have their picture made with the governor. And I'll tell you a secret: I use it to get people out of my office. When time runs out, I'm like, hey, how'd you like to get a picture in front of the Great Seal? And then they're halfway out the door."

He led us into a dark-paneled office with a big desk and a long shiny table and leather-covered swivel chairs.

"And here's my office. You can sit behind the desk if you like. I do some work at the desk, but mostly it's a place for eating cookies. The real work is over here, at the table, talking to people. You want to sit behind the desk?"

"Thanks, Governor, but I don't want to take up too much of your time," I said. "Let's go straight to the table."

"I'm sitting at the desk!" Martinez exclaimed, and went straight for the governor's chair. King, Taleesa, and I sat at the table.

"So what are your impressions so far?" King asked me. "What do you think of the capitol?"

"Honestly, Governor, I think I like you a lot more than I expected to," I said.

King leaned back with a smile. "Well, I'm a politician. It's my job to make people like me."

"Well, here's something that would make me like you even more. Call off the hunt for the alligator in Dead Beaver Swamp," I said.

"Go on," he said. "I know you have a case you want to make. Lay it out."

I went through everything. As governor, he had the power to start or stop the hunt for the gator. Gators almost never bit people in Alabama, so there wasn't a lot of past experience to go by. But there was no reason to think the so-called Swamp Monster was a danger to anybody unless they were dumb enough to actually chase down the gator.

"They do this in Florida," I said. "A gator bites someone, so they go on a gator hunt. The first big gator they find, bigger than six feet, they kill it. And they claim they got the gator that bit. Even though they have no way of knowing they got the right gator. It's just pointless killing."

"I don't know," King said, no longer smiling. "I don't know if it's pointless. It makes people feel better. It makes them feel safe."

"But does it actually make them safe?" I asked. "People are safe when they respect the gators that are there. When they know a gator's there, and they stay out of the water. What happens if you kill a gator, and claim you got the Swamp Monster, and some other idiot goes swimming in the swamp? Surely if there's one gator in there, there's more than one."

A tall, red-haired woman stepped into the room. "I've got your proclamation, Governor," she said, and handed him a picture frame with a piece of paper in it.

King brightened again. "Ah, the moment I've been waiting for. Atty, I called you here to give you this gift. In honor of your activism for kindness to animals, and in respect for your admirable abilities in the law, I hereby appoint you as an honorary colonel, aide-de-camp in the Alabama State Militia."

He handed me the picture frame. There it was, the same thing he said, but printed in calligraphy on a yellow sheet of paper, with a painting of the Great Seal of Alabama. It looked like a page in some medieval book, but there was my name: "Lt. Col. Atticus T. Peale."

"Wow," I said. "Governor, this is really nice. I'm honored."

"No fair!" said Martinez, rocking in the governor's chair. "I was part of all this. I want to be a colonel, too."

"I'm so sorry, Martinez," the governor said. "I didn't know you were coming. Jen, how long will it take to make this young man an admiral?"

"I'll be back with it in a minute, sir," Jen said.

"Look at him now," King said. "Your brother. I made his day. This is what I love about this job, having the power to help people. Maybe you'll be in this same place one day, Atty. I don't doubt it."

"Governor, with all due respect, I'm all about helping people now," I said. "And, you know, you have it in your power to call off this cruel hunt and educate people about the dangers of provoking alligators. All you have to do is give the word."

King sighed.

"Atty, you'd be surprised," he said. "You'd be surprised at how little power I really do have sometimes. If the legislature doesn't like me, I can't do anything. If the voters don't like me, I don't even have a job. And when people are afraid for their safety, it's not time for me to experiment with new policies. I have to do what I can to make people feel safe. One day you'll be in this job, or one like it, and you'll see."

I shook my head. "Governor, you said it's your job to make people like you. And I do, Governor, I do like you a lot. But I'm not sure that really is your job. And I don't ever expect to be in your position. I'd like it if people liked me. But there are more important things than being liked."

"Atty," Taleesa scolded, in a stage whisper.

The governor looked wounded, for just a moment, and I felt like a jerk. But then he brightened again.

"Who'd like to get their picture made in front of the Great Seal?" he said.

"An admiral outranks a colonel," Martinez said. We were walking through the capitol dome, behind Jen Carter, the red-haired woman who worked for the governor. She had just shown us the room where the legislature voted to secede in 1861. Now she was pointing up at the inside of the capitol dome, which was a gorgeous pink, painted over with pictures of slaves loading cotton bales onto a boat and white people riding horses in front of a mansion with columns. The only person not looking up was Martinez, who had his phone out, frantically reading everything he could about the powers of a high-ranking naval officer.

"Dang," he said. "They didn't say anything about me being an admiral."

"They who?" I said, still looking up.

"Look." Martinez handed me the phone. "I'm in the picture, but no admiral."

He was reading the website of the governor's office. They already had a story up about our visit. Photos of me and Martinez with King, in front of the Great Seal.

GOVERNOR HONORS YOUNG ACTIVIST

Alabama Gov. Fischer King honored young activist Atticus Peale, 12, as an honorary colonel during a visit to the Alabama State Capitol today.

"Miss Peale, who is now Col. Peale, is a wonderful example of the kind of civic engagement that made Alabama the great state it is today," Gov. King said.

Miss Peale and her brother, Martinez, are volunteers at the Strudwick County Animal Shelter, and have produced a series of YouTube videos and newspaper

articles to promote pet adoption. She
also wrote the governor recently about
his decision to direct state employees to
capture and kill the alligator known to
Strudwick County residents as the "Swamp
Monster." The Swamp Monster recently
attacked and maimed a Houmahatchee
man, and local residents tell of a long
history of attacks by the creature.

"Col. Peale and I had a frank
discussion about the Swamp Monster,
and I think we came to substantial
agreement that something has to be
done to keep the citizens of this state
safe," Gov. King said. "I'm proud to
call her my good friend."

"Aaaah!" I shouted. It echoed through the dome. A group
of fourth-graders, on the other side of the capitol dome, all
stared at me.

"How can he say this?" I whispered to Martinez. "We
didn't agree to anything! This didn't happen."

"Is everything okay?" Jen Carter asked.

I wanted to say, no, your boss is a dirty sack of donkey
poop. Something inside me, that Taleesa voice I hear in my
head even when she's not around, told me to just be chill
and nod my head. "Some people don't get to throw tan-
trums," Taleesa often says to me, in her sad, wise Milwaukee
voice. I'll never know the whole story about where that voice
comes from, but I've heard her talk about walking for miles

in the snow looking for Old Martinez, her only real parent, when he went missing. I remember her speech at the PTO meeting, when she got all teary-eyed about librarians and how they would not only give a kid a book, but also feed them and listen to their problems and give a kid a place to stay during the day when there was nowhere else to go.

So I waited. We saw the Old House Chamber, with its big silver stove and a plaque honoring the vote to leave the Union. We saw giant portraits of George and Lurleen Wallace. For some reason I got the feeling that both of the paintings were about to fall right on top of us. And then Jen Carter dropped us off at the Goat Hill Store, a capitol gift shop full of books about the Creek War and the Civil War, models of the capitol and dolls in hoopskirts. I kept a polite smile on my face right up until the moment we stepped out of the gift shop and back onto the street.

"Effing coward!" I said, stuffing my honorary colonel certificate, frame and all, into a sidewalk garbage can. "This was all a sham! He didn't want to talk! He just wanted to shut me down."

"Welcome to Montgomery," Taleesa said.

"How can he sit there and say he doesn't have the power to do anything? He's the most powerful person in the state. And then to turn around and make it look like we cut a deal," I said.

"Atty, you're an activist," Taleesa said. "And he's a politician. They look like the same thing sometimes, but they're not. You're about changing the world, and he's about running it. Some people speak out because they care about others, and some people speak out because they want to be heard themselves. And some people can't tell the difference. Those are the politicians. I think you were expecting to meet an activist, and he was expecting to meet a politician. And I think he probably thought he was letting you win, at least a little."

"I haven't won anything," I said. "Dismissed in court and dissed by the governor."

"Oh, I don't think you were dissed," Taleesa said. "Look, lots of people, grown-up, powerful people like Backsley Graddoch, would love to have their picture taken with the governor. They'd hang it up on their wall. Because they're interested in power, and being a friend of the governor will make them more powerful. So I think he thinks he gave you something big."

As we walked, Martinez continued to gaze at his admiral certificate.

"Give, nothing," he said. "I earned this. Look, it says right here: 'For his moral courage and exemplary service to the State of Alabama . . .' See there? I *earned* being an admiral."

"Oooh," I said. "Mine didn't say 'courage.' I wanna see."

Martinez drew back. "Stay away from my certificate, you ex-colonel, you. You're not touching mine. Mine's going up on the wall."

The ride back home was quiet, but I don't really think any of us noticed. Taleesa was already thinking about an upcoming story—she mumbled a little to herself the way she does when she's writing—and Martinez was on his phone still reading about admirals.

"Mom," he said, about halfway home. "Can I get a bosun's whistle?"

I was just quiet. Stuck. Nowhere for my mind to race to. *Bing.*

Princess_P: You lose again. Take a look at WSFA.

I logged on to the TV station's website.

```
MONSTER GATOR DESTROYED
IN STRUDWICK COUNTY

HOUMAHATCHEE—The Swamp Monster is
dead.
   Private alligator hunters, working
under contract with Alabama Fish and
Wildlife, trapped and killed an 11-foot
alligator in Dead Beaver Swamp near
Houmahatchee this morning, sheriff's
deputies report.
   After examining the contents of the
animal's stomach, hunters concluded
that it's the same gator that attacked a
Strudwick County man last week.
   "They found a human hand still inside
the gator," said Deputy Troy Butler.
```

There was a picture of a big bull gator on the back of a truck, one little gator-arm hanging limply over the tailgate, and a bunch of guys standing in the truck bed, each with one foot on the gator's back. The story told about the "struggle" with the gator, which they apparently shot in the back of the head, and then lots of quotes from the gator hunters about how "some misguided individuals" don't understand the dangers of aggressive gators. At first I thought they were talking about the dangers of going into the swamp at night, but then I realized all of this was aimed at me and my campaign to save the Monster.

> **Princess_P:** You're a freak like your mother. High school will be hell for you. You don't belong here. You'll end like her.

That made me mad.

> **atticustpeale:** I know who you are.

I was bluffing, of course. It was several minutes before she wrote back.

> **Princess_P:** Who am I then?

I had nothing to say. I put down the phone and let it ding, again and again. And when we got home, even though it was still light out, I went straight to bed.

It was dark, I don't know how many hours later. I felt the weight of someone sitting on the bed. I thought it was Taleesa, but it was Dad.

"Atty," he said. "I heard you went to bed early. Are you okay? Do you feel okay?"

"I'm just tired," I said.

"I know things didn't go well with the alligator case. Do you want to talk about it?"

"I want to sleep," I said. "I just need to sleep. For a long time."

"It's almost sunrise," Dad said. "I'm getting ready for work. Do you want breakfast?"

"Sleep, I want to sleep," I said. "If I can just sleep longer I'll be fine. I'm not going to the animal shelter. I'm catching up on my sleep."

Dad was silent for a long time. Taleesa came to the door. "She's almost a teenager, Paul. It's normal."

And then I swirled back down into black, dreamless sleep again.

Then came brightness, color. A voice.

"Get up!" Someone yanked the covers right off my bed.

It was Megg, of all people. In my bedroom, in her animal shelter uniform. It was mid-morning: the sun was squinty-bright. In the next room, on TV, I could hear cartoon superheroes trash-talking each other.

"Get out of bed, Colonel Peale," Megg said. "You made an agreement. You'd work for me until the end of the summer. No skipping work. It's 10 a.m. You're late."

"Everybody gets a sick day now and again," I said.

"Are you sick? Do you do have the flu?"

"Not that kind of sick," I said.

"Are you getting your period?" she asked.

"Lord, no," I said. That thing! People always want to talk about that thing, about "becoming a woman" and dating boys and all that. Even after I become a woman, I intend to pretend all that isn't happening. "Stop talking about it. You're depressing me."

"Are you depressed then?" Megg said. "Is that it? Because if you are, we'll go to the doctor right now."

That irked me.

"Don't talk to me about depression," I said. "What do you know about it? You don't know anything about depression."

"Look at me," Megg said.

I looked into her eyes. Her round face, her close-cropped hair. I thought about the yellowed photos in the halls of her house. A young Megg, getting married. Megg and her kids with countless dogs, dogs now buried in the back yard.

"Okay," I said. "I withdraw the question."

"Get your shoes on. It's good that you slept in your clothes. I've got just one job for you today, and you can get right on it."

We left Martinez in front of the TV and rode to the animal shelter in silence, me still in my rumpled dress from the day before. As we walked into the shelter, one of the teenage volunteers saw me and did a half-hearted little salute. "Colonel," she said in greeting. I tried to smile back.

Megg led me through her office into the back rooms with tile walls and the stainless steel table, where the vet treats the dogs. That place makes me nervous.

"I'm going to show you what I did at work this morning, while you were sleeping," Megg said. Now I was really nervous.

Megg pushed open a door. Another tiled room. And there, lined up on the floor, were a dozen dogs. Beagles, Labradors, a mutt that looked like a dingo. No puppies, but a couple just past the puppy stage. All lying on their sides as if asleep. All dead.

"This is what I did this morning while you were asleep," Megg said. "I put down all these sweet animals, because no one would take them."

When I finally caught my breath, I started bawling. "Why are you showing me this, Megg?" I said. "This is hateful. You're just being mean."

Megg got down on her knees, held me by the shoulders, looked me in the eye.

"Atty, this is half as many as I was putting down every month before you and your brother came to work for me," Megg said. "The videos, the newspaper articles, they've worked. People have come from all over to adopt our dogs and cats. Look at them: for each one of the dogs that's lying there, there's another one that's alive because of you. Honestly, I don't know how I'm going to manage when the summer ends and you go back to school, and it's coming soon.

"Look, Atty," she continued. "You can be sad if you want to. If you try things, you have setbacks, sometimes you even get embarrassed in public. If you feel demoralized, that's okay. But you can't stop doing what you do. You can't ever decide not to go on, because someone is depending on you to do what you do, every day."

We sat there and cried for a long time. I don't really know why. The gator situation wasn't any sadder than the stuff Megg dealt with every day, and I have no idea why some things set off a crying jag and others don't. Maybe life just has a certain amount of sadness in it, and you just have to cry from time to time to let it out.

Whatever was going on, in a few minutes I felt better. Megg offered to take me home. Instead, I called home and asked Taleesa if she'd bring me a change of clothes.

I had cages to clean and pets to feed.

11

I have a riddle for you.

A little boy lives in a trailer outside of Hayneville. He's poor. No cell phone, no Internet, no cable TV, no toys except a few Happy Meal rejects. One Christmas his cousin gives him some chicken wire and lumber and a baby chick inside a cardboard box. The boy works all Christmas day to put together a little chicken coop, and from then on the chicken is his best friend. He loves it, and he spends hours petting it, watching it, following it around the yard.

One night, the boy hears cackling and growling from the chicken house. He grabs a flashlight and his dad's .410 shotgun, and he goes out to see what's happening. There's a fox, a beautiful red flash of a fox, trying to get into the chicken house.

Of course the boy shoots the fox. That's not my riddle.

The riddle is, why is the chicken a beloved pet, and why is the fox dead? You love your dog, so you put food in its bowl.

Who loved the animal that's in your dog's bowl? When a baby chick pulls his first wriggling worm out of the ground, whose side should I be on?

I can't answer that question. But I did think about it a lot over the last few weeks of my summer at the animal shelter. Those big bags of cat food clearly say "made with real chicken," and it bothered me that when I fed a cat, I was feeding it a chicken, just like the chicken in my riddle. Why wasn't the chicken a pet? How would the cat live if we spared the chicken?

It's something you could think about on a mountaintop for years, but I didn't have years or a mountaintop, so I threw myself into work. I put away the "Colonel Peale" dress and didn't think about filing another legal brief. I kept the cages cleaner than they'd ever been. I organized the storeroom. I convinced Taleesa to buy me some paint, and I touched up the sign in front of the shelter, something Miss Megg told me only a county employee was allowed to do, though she wouldn't tell if I wouldn't.

And of course I kept on writing profiles of pets for the *Herald*. The week after my meeting with the governor, one of the Braxtons put up my column with the byline "Col. Atticus Peale." They thought it was cute. I put a stop to it.

Thinking about my riddle was a good way to avoid that other riddle, the one that can't be solved: seventh grade. The days were ticking down and I just didn't want to deal with it.

School and I just don't get along. I'll be honest with you: I don't get along with the *kids* at school, really. I guess it all goes back to the early days, to the years of tea parties and playing princess.

Other girls never liked playing princess with me, because I have the whole Cinderella thing figured out. I always thought it was kind of dumb that the fairy godmother gives Cinderella stuff that lasts only until midnight, and I always thought that if I were Cinderella I'd interrupt the fairy godmother—I'm bad to interrupt people—and ask to be bitten by a radioactive spider instead.

Then I'd be Spiderella, in a beautiful spider-silk gown, swinging through the capital with the proportional strength of a spider. I'd live with my stepmom and keep my secret identity, while saving the kingdom and dating the prince at night. Martinez liked it, as long as he didn't have to play the prince. But other girls got really tired of their tea parties being busted up by supervillains.

Mermaids were a problem, too. I love the idea of mermaids. To be a superhero of sorts, a fish-lady, except that you have the face and hair of Peyton Vebelstadt. That's just about perfect. But in the cartoons, all mermaids seem to do is sit around on rocks combing their hair with seashells.

Then one day Martinez came home with an action figure, a Navy frogman, and I realized there was something better than a mermaid. I mean, what a beautiful word, "frogman." Even though it isn't what it sounds like. A frogman is, like, a really tough soldier guy in a wet suit with flippers, who plants bombs on the bottom of ships, and defuses bombs, and carries a cool-looking speargun.

That gave me a new idea: frogmaids. Half-fish, half lovely girl, all adventure. Spearguns and utility vests instead of clamshell bikinis. Exploring caves, fighting polluters, having tea parties. Much better. I tried to recruit girls into my

Frogmaid Corps, but none of them could handle the tough discipline involved. Peyton Vebelstadt was one of the first to drop out. Shameka Vinson was the last. She told me I was too bossy.

I know, "bossy" is a bad word. One of our teachers tried to put a stop to it. In fifth grade, Ms. Johnson started the year with a "Ban Bossy" on her bulletin board, with biographies of women who were generals or who ran countries and so on. After about a month, she took it down and put up a billboard about speaking to each other with respect. I kind of got the feeling that I was the one to blame for that.

"Atty's a very smart, very capable student," Ms. Johnson said to Taleesa at our parent-teacher conference. "But she's also what we call a shout-out. When she knows the answer, and she knows a lot of answers, she just blurts it out before anyone else can." Then she turned to me. "Atty, when you do this, you're taking away the other kids' chances to learn and—"

"If I was good at hitting a ball, you wouldn't tell me I was ruining the game for everybody else," I said.

"And that's another thing," Ms. Johnson said. "Interrupting people is rude. You need to find a way not to do that."

I'll say this: Mrs. Johnson did listen to my comment about hitting a ball. She tried to get me into Genius Bowl, the big academic trivia contest where blurting out the answers and interrupting people are actually good things. But I didn't join for deeply personal reasons.

Premsyl Svoboda, my one and only ex-boyfriend, was the captain of the Genius Bowl team.

Premsyl broke my heart. In first grade, he was a new

immigrant from the Czech Republic, and he didn't know a word of English. Our teacher paired me up with him, to guide him around the school and teach him about English words and American customs. Mrs. Frist, the first-grade teacher, said I was the natural choice, because I was from an "intelligent, cross-cultural family" and should know how to reach out to someone who speaks only Czech. Which shows how much she knows.

I taught Premsyl everything about America. All the important rules. *Nobody likes a snitch. Boyfriends come up with pet names for their girlfriends in their native language, and they always hold your hand at the lunch table. American men can take their wife's name.* (So if I'm writing "Atty Svoboda" on my notebook, he should write "Premsyl Peale" on his.)

Mrs. Frist took Premsyl away from me. Because he asked. That's right. My boyfriend didn't break up with me directly, he *went to the teacher* and asked for permission to break up with me. And then I got in trouble for teaching Premsyl a bunch of rules about American culture that don't really exist, though they should.

"If an adult did some of the things Atty did, she'd probably be charged with fraud," Mrs. Frist told my dad.

So this is what I faced, going into the seventh grade. Seventh grade, which every credible psychologist said was a meat grinder that turns confident young women into self-doubting chain-smokers.

Peyton Vebelstadt would be there, Premsyl would be there, Shameka would be there, everybody. The cast of the sad drama of my school life so far.

And one of them, almost certainly, was Princess P.

Dad wasn't having a great time, either. I knew because I read about it in the Houmahatchee *Herald*.

BEFORE MURDER, LOTTERY WINNER HAD
CHANGE OF HEART
by Rickie Braxton

The Sunday before someone shot him
dead, Jefferson Davis Ambrose had a
religious awakening.

Ambrose, a local pawnshop owner, was
already a member in good standing at
Red Creek First Baptist. He was also
known as a penny-pincher—"Heatmiser"
was his nickname because he refused to
turn on air-conditioning in his store—
and as a hard-driving businessman.
He was also, much to the chagrin of
his pastor, a regular player of the
Florida Lottery, known for his regular
trips across the state line to pick his
favorite numbers.

But on one Sunday in May, with a
lottery ticket still in his back pocket,
Jeff Ambrose came down the aisle of
the church when pastor Michael Jones
called. Ambrose, 64, said he'd never
really known salvation, and wanted to
change his life.

"He had tears streaming down his

face," Jones said. "He said that as soon as he had the money, he'd get out of the pawnshop business and devote all his time to doing the Lord's work."

What followed was a bizarre chain of events that seemed to be straight out of a Hollywood movie. In that Sunday night's Florida Lottery drawing, Ambrose's ticket came out a winner. He wouldn't take home the biggest Lotto jackpot, but he hit all the numbers in the Fantasy Five and was set to take home $225,000.

Ambrose told his pastor that he'd use the money to close down his store and retire. He even had plans to return pawned items to some of his more financially troubled customers to show his change of heart.

"We ask God to forgive our debts as we forgive our debtors," Jones said. "He said he didn't have much time left, and lots of debt to forgive."

Friends told Ambrose to keep the lottery win a secret, at least until he'd collected the money. But it didn't stay secret for long. On Monday morning, Ambrose stopped for breakfast at the Speedy Queen on Galvez Road and told the whole story to everyone who would listen—about his conversion experience, his lottery win, and his plan to close his pawnshop.

"I'd never seen him like that," said Annie Smith, a waitress at the Speedy Queen who regularly served Ambrose. "He was bright and happy, like a little boy. I wasn't sure how much of it was the Lord and how much of it was winning the lottery."

Smith said she assumed he'd won the big lottery prize, about $12 million, not a lesser jackpot. And she was impressed when he pulled the lottery ticket out of his wallet and showed it to her.

Police say Ambrose called at least two customers early Monday morning and told them to collect their items free of charge. One of those customers arrived to find Ambrose dead in the pawn shop's back office, his winning ticket gone.

Police later found the ticket, and a gun that matched the bullet in Ambrose's body, in the possession of Jethro Gersham, 55, a disabled man who lived near the Speedy Queen. Gersham was a customer of Ambrose's—he'd pawned the very gun that was later used to kill the pawnshop owner—and was often known to hang out in the Speedy Queen parking lot, chatting with customers.

"He used to come around all the time," Smith said. "Then a few weeks before the shooting, he and J.D. got in a big argument in the parking lot. J.D. called Jethro a deadbeat and Jethro called J.D. a greedy you-know-what."

Police believe Gersham found out about the lottery ticket and came into the pawnshop claiming to have the money he needed to get his gun back. Then he shot Gersham and took both the gun and the lottery ticket, police say.

In fact, police say they have a confession, signed by Gersham, that confirms that's how it happened.

Gersham's attorney, Paul Peale, says the police tricked Gersham into signing the confession. Gersham is illiterate, Peale said, and didn't know what he was signing.

Peale said police should look more deeply into Gersham's version of the story. When first caught by police, Gersham said he was given the gun by a man in a red hat—not Ambrose—who worked at the store. Gersham's story doesn't explain how he got the lottery ticket;

```
the defendant claims the man in the red
hat gave him only a receipt for the gun.
    Ambrose didn't have any employees at
the pawnshop, though the co-owner, his
brother-in-law, often worked behind the
counter when Ambrose wasn't around.
Police say the brother-in-law was fishing
the day of the killing, and has a
receipt from a marina to prove it.
    Sources close to the case say Peale is
working frantically to get Gersham a plea
deal that will send his client to prison
but avoid death by lethal injection.
Peale declined to comment on the issue,
citing attorney-client privilege.
```

When I read it, I heaved a big sigh. I know Dad would probably like me to grow up to be a lawyer like him. But if this is what it takes, I don't know. How can you defend somebody, somebody you know to be innocent, and still help him plead guilty? I know Dad's job was to do what's best for his client, and I guess I can see where Jethro would rather go to prison for six or seven years—instead of life in prison, or getting executed—if it didn't look like he could win. But how can a person go to jail for something as horrible as murder without even going to a courtroom and explaining their side of the story?

"You know I can't talk to you about the case, Atty," Dad told me. "But let me just plant an idea in your head. Better yet, let me ask you a question. Who taught you to read?"

"Nobody," I said. "I've always been able to read. Even in kindergarten."

It was true, or I thought it was. My earliest memories are of when Taleesa and Martinez first came into our lives. I remember crying because Martinez got to sit in the seat in the grocery cart. Suddenly I was too old to ride the coin-operated giraffe outside of Super-Valu because I was the big girl now, and I didn't get to do little kid stuff. But even then, in my earliest memories, I could walk down the aisle of the store and point and read names. Tide, Bounty, OxiClean. People would stop and smile and tell me how amazingly smart I was, so I kept doing it, and did it louder. Reading is my superpower.

"So who taught you?" Dad asked again.

"Nobody," I said. "Okay, you. Or Taleesa. Mom? Did Mom teach me to read?"

Dad paused, and sighed. "Do you remember a woman named Molly? Sometimes she went by Menolly, a nickname. It's from a book."

"*Dragonsong*," I said. "I've read it. I love that book."

"The copy that's on our shelf now? First printing, with the flying dragon on the cover? Molly gave your mom that book. Do you remember Molly at all?"

"Never heard of her," I said.

"You used to sit on her lap right there in the living room, reading picture books," Dad said. "For hours. You were a toddler. And she would point to letters and sound them out. For hours at a time. Because you'd let her. After your mom died, and before I met Taleesa, she came around every day. First to help me, then really just to see you. Every day."

"Why don't I remember her?" I asked.

"Things got weird," Dad said. "I really needed her. You really needed her. I love her like a sister. I miss her a lot. But she wanted . . . I don't know. She wanted more. She told me she was in love with me. I really wasn't ready for that. Honestly I hadn't even thought about her in that way until she said it. I was just taking and taking from her and never even asked why she wanted to give. So she left. I mean, really left. Not a call. Not another visit." Dad sighed again.

"Just what I needed," I said. "More guilt. This woman taught me to read, and I don't even know her." I paused for a minute, then: "What the heck does this have to do with Jethro?"

"Atty, you and I have been watched over by the grace of others our whole lives," Dad said. "We don't even know all the people we need to thank for what we have. But Jethro, he didn't have a Molly. He can't read. Even the school system that was supposed to teach him to read, it didn't do that. I can't see any bitterness in him about that. But I can see why he doesn't trust public institutions to do what they say they're going to do. If the schools will let him sit there for nine years and not teach him, if the cops will make him sign a confession they know he doesn't understand, why would he trust the court to give him a fair trial? And if you don't believe you can get a fair trial, why wouldn't you take a deal for a few years in prison, compared to execution?"

I shook my head. "Doesn't anything work the way it's supposed to?" I said. "Doesn't anything work in real life the way it works on TV?"

"Football does, I guess," Dad said.

That didn't make me feel better at all.

12

It was strange, going to school without Martinez. For all those years at the elementary school, he was like a parrot on my shoulder. *He* got nervous about the first day of school. *He* was bummed that he couldn't play video games all day anymore. *He* knew which kids at school were the bullies and the tattletales, and he dreaded seeing them. And he would chatter about it every morning, as Taleesa dropped us off at Houmahatchee Elementary. As the big sister, I was the one who had to calm him down, the one who had to make sure his lunch wasn't poking out of his backpack, the one who warned him his britches weren't zipped. (Martinez hates the word "britches," which Dad uses from time to time. Dad, and grizzled old prospectors in Westerns. And me, sometimes, because it annoys Martinez.)

Now we were driving to Houmahatchee High, a place where twelve-year-olds like me would wander the halls alongside seniors with mustaches and sophomores in Air Force

ROTC uniforms. Suddenly I realized that, for all those years, taking care of Martinez kept me from being scared myself.

"Why do you keep checking your fly?" Taleesa asked. "Is something going on down there? You know, it's almost time for all those changes that turn a girl into—"

"STOP!" I said. "Just stop, T. Don't make this whole thing any weirder than it is."

I can't remember when I didn't know about the birds and the bees, because my parents believe in "being frank and honest" and they talk all the time about how all this realistic information will keep me from getting pregnant in high school. And they are totally correct. I am never getting pregnant. I am never ever doing any of that.

"You're already sounding like a teenager," Taleesa said.

"Uuugh," I replied, realizing suddenly that I did sound just like a teenager in some dumb sitcom. But why couldn't she see that it wasn't me that was changing? It was circumstances that were changing. One minute I'm doing my real life's work, darn near running the animal shelter, and the next minute I'm thrust into Teen World against my choice. I wanted to say this so much but somehow it just came out as a big ball of frustration. "Uuugh."

Martinez didn't have any problem when we dropped him off at Houmahatchee Elementary.

"With Atty gone, now I can assert my rightful kingship over this place," he said as we pulled in to the drop-off. "So long, great oppressor."

"So long, Britches," I shouted as he got out of the car.

"I've got ninety-nine problems," he shot back, but I pulled the door shut before he could finish.

And then we pulled up to Houmahatchee High, a big chunk of cinder-block building. The building was new, just finished last year, but it looked spookily familiar.

"This thing looks just like the county jail," I said. "It looks like a big nursing home where people go to watch *Wheel of Fortune* and die."

"Check yourself before you poke fun," Taleesa said. "You don't have any idea what people are doing in their free time at a nursing home. It's okay to be crotchety and grumpy at twelve, but don't go projecting it on somebody you never met."

Adding to the jailhouse atmosphere, there was a deputy standing outside, the school resource officer. I felt a little twinge when I saw the car and the uniform, but as we pulled closer it was clear it was definitely *not* Troy Butler, but some older balding guy who smiled and waved at everybody. Probably retired.

The guy standing next to the resource officer wasn't in uniform, but he seemed a lot more like a cop. Aviator glasses, a little bushy mustache, three-piece suit, with a big radio in one hand. As we pulled up I could see him stopping some of the taller boys and looking close at them to see if they'd shaved properly.

"I guess that's Dr. Dalton, the vice principal," Taleesa said. "Looks like he's the disciplinarian. Good luck."

I got out, hoisted my backpack over my shoulder, and headed for the door of the school. At first, Dalton didn't notice me—he was busy telling some girl her dress was too short—and I tiptoed past. But just as I reached for the door: "Young lady," he said. "Come here, my friend."

I turned. The aviator glasses were looking me up and down. Creepy. So I looked right back at him the same way.

"Are you going to go all the way into school without saying hello?" he said. "Is that polite and respectful? Is that the Purple Devil way?"

So we're doing this.

"I'm sorry, hello." I stuck out my hand. "I'm—"

"Let me make something really clear from the outset," Dalton said. "We have rules here. Purple Devils are polite. You'll always say hello. You'll always acknowledge when someone else is there. You'll always lend a hand."

I nodded. I'm a smart aleck, but I know when to keep my mouth shut.

"And you'll wear a belt. That's in the dress code, for young men and young women. We went over this at orientation, so you know this."

"I missed orientation," I said. "I know it's strange, but my mom's a writer and she's bad to forget stuff when she's working."

"Purple Devils don't make excuses," he said. "You're in high school now. Seventh grade, but high school. You're becoming an adult, and you need to take responsibility for your actions, not blame your parents. Now give me a 341."

"A what?"

Dalton sighed, reached into his pocket and pulled out three folded-up slips of paper. "Each of these is a Form 341. You carry three of them around in your right front shirt pocket. You're supposed to wear a shirt with a front pocket. Every time I see you commit an infraction, I can ask you for a 341. When you have none left, or when you lose your 341s, that's a trip to the office. Understood?"

"Understood." I turned to leave. "Why is it called a 341?"

"It's based on Air Force Form 341," he said. "The military uses it in basic training. And, here, since you don't have one, is a copy of the Houmahatchee Code of Conduct. Now: aren't you going to say hello?"

All right, I thought, *time to turn on the lawyer stuff.* I thrust my hand out.

"Atticus T. Peale, pleased to meet you," I said.

And just like that, the angry-cop face went away.

"Atticus . . . hey, you're Colonel Peale," he said, suddenly bright and almost chummy. "You're friends with Governor King."

"We've met," I said. "I wouldn't say we're close."

"Well, I'm a big fan of Governor King," he said. "It's good to have a strong conservative man in charge. What's he like in person?"

I shrugged.

"He likes cookies," I said. "He doesn't like alligators."

Dalton's face clouded over again. Guess I shouldn't have been so flippant about it.

"Well, a lot of people would love to have his ear," Dalton said. "A lot of people who *don't* have connections in the political world. You're lucky to get to meet him."

And that was my introduction to seventh grade. There, see what I mean? Seventh-graders live in a madhouse run by madmen. We're not crazy, and we're not going through a phase. I'd like to see Backsley Graddoch running around with 341s in his front pocket. Imagine how he'd behave!

Inside the school lobby, there was a giant mural of a sinister-looking purple demon with a football in one hand and a pitchfork in the other. And next to him, in bold letters, the Houmahatchee Code of Conduct:

Purple Devils are Honest.
Purple Devils are Sweet.
Purple Devils are Decorous.
Purple Devils Look Up Words They Don't Know.
Purple Devils Respect Tradition.
Purple Devils are Humble.

And on and on. There were maybe fifty items. I hoped they wouldn't ask us to remember them all.

I pulled a crumpled sheet out of my pocket. When we missed orientation, the school district mailed us a nastygram with my locker number on it and the name of my homeroom teacher, Ms. Pinson. So, let's find this locker.

As I headed down the hall, I realized something: I was scared. Genuinely scared. Facing judges and governors never was all that hard. Other kids, though, that was hard. They're all so handsome and pretty, they laugh and say funny things, and I never feel like I really get what's going on in their heads. I want to say cool, fun things, too, but my head just isn't in the same place.

In the hallway, I saw a lot of new faces. Skater boys looking awkward without their boards. Beefy rednecks with crooked smiles and camouflage jackets. Tall volleyball girls who looked like they could jump across the Grand Canyon and still land on Barbie-doll tiptoes.

And Premsyl Svoboda. Leaning against his locker, talking to some girl with big glasses who clutched her books against her chest and laughed with big, braces-covered teeth. Whoever she was, she liked him, and he knew it. And it wasn't hard to see why. He was taller now, with his blond hair in a cool, floppy cut. He looked very ready for high school.

I looked at my locker number and groaned. No. 622. Premsyl was leaning on locker number 623.

"Hey, Premsyl," I said.

"Hey, Atty," he said.

"Pretzel?" chuckled Braces Girl. "Did she just call you Pretzel?"

"Only my mom calls me that now, Atty," Premsyl said. "The kids on the Genius Bowl team call me P.J."

"P.J. is like the *king* of Genius Bowl, aren't you?" Braces Girl said.

"I wouldn't be if Atty were on the team," Premsyl said. "She's super smart. You could join, Atty."

"I probably won't have time," I said. "I go straight to the animal shelter after work. Lots and lots to do."

"Oh, yeah," Premsyl said. "Colonel Peale. You're the animal activist now."

"Please do not call me Colonel," I said. "Some of us like our original names just fine."

"Oh," said Braces Girl. "So this is *her*. This is the one you told me about. She's the one who thinks she's a lawyer."

I really thought Braces Girl seemed sweet at first. She probably was, usually. But now that I'd butted in to her talk with Premsyl, she was just full-on catty. And I realized I was feeling catty, too.

I took a deep breath. *Come on, Atty, think like a lawyer.*

"Look, y'all, I see where this is going," I said. "Premsyl, you've become really cute. Your accent is great. And, yes, your name is Premsyl and, yes, you're my ex-boyfriend." I turned to Braces Girl. "But Premsyl has already rejected me, and I'm not going to get into some kind of competition with you about it. I'm just here because it's my locker he's leaning on. So I'll just get in and out."

Braces Girl blushed. "I don't know where you get off. I'm not hitting on P.J. I'm just having a conversation."

"Well, P.J.'s hitting on you," I said. "Be good, Premsyl. If you break her heart, I'll break your face."

And off to class. *That went well*, I thought. And yet, in my gut, I knew it didn't go well. No matter what you say in high school, it's going to be wrong somehow.

Into Ms. Pinson's classroom. The first thing I saw was twenty-five faces suddenly looking up at me. Everybody had already arrived, and they were all clustered in groups: future cheerleaders, the girls who love horses, gamer guys, and so on. There were maybe three desks available. Everybody seemed to be watching to see which one I'd choose.

None of my old elementary-school friends were there. Not Venetia and Sam, the girls I used to jump rope with. Mia the Spelling Bee Goddess was in private school this year. I noticed Peyton Vebelstadt, lanky and beautiful as ever, sitting with the future-cheerleader types. I waved.

"Hey, Peyton," I said. "How's the cat?"

Peyton looked at me with her eyebrows furrowed and waved half-heartedly. Some girl whispered something into her ear and they giggled together. Then she looked back at me, again seeming worried.

Ah, well. Guess I won't sit next to her.

In the back of the room, some girl was slumped over her desk, seemingly asleep. Black leather jacket, uncombed mass of black hair. If she was asleep, I guess she wouldn't mind me taking the desk in front of her.

Ms. Pinson stood up and started taking roll. I guessed she was the biology teacher: I couldn't take my eyes off the grody "visible man" model she stood next to, a rubber dummy with rubber-dummy liver and intestines just hanging out there like anybody's business.

During roll call, I always wish my last name started with *A*. Why is it so nerve-racking to wait for your name to be called?

"Atticus Peale," Mrs. Pinson called, finally.

"Here."

She squinted at me. "You're Atticus?"

"Atty for short," I said. I saw her mouth the word "female" as she wrote something in her attendance book.

"Okay, Atticus Peale. Reagan Royall," Mrs. Pinson looked around the room eagerly. "Reagan Royall?"

The sleeping girl behind me looked up, wiping drool off the corner of her mouth. "Syeah?" she said, with a sultry detached tone. She had really been asleep. As she tossed her head, I could see a bright pink stripe down the middle of her black mane of hair. Give her a chance to comb it, and it would look very punk.

"Miss Royall," the teacher said. "Am I seeking pink hair?"

"I like to think of it as purple," Reagan Royall said.

"You realize that's not permitted by the dress code," Mrs. Pinson said. "We went over this in orientation. Purple Devils don't have purple hair."

I snorted. Couldn't help it. "Well, technically," I said. "Purple Devils are purple."

"Miss Peale, do you have your copy of the Code of Conduct? Open it up to the first two pages."

I dug into my backpack and got the book out. On the first two pages, dozens of PURPLE DEVIL statements. I scanned down and there it was:

48. PURPLE DEVILS WEAR SKIRTS BELOW THE KNEE
49. PURPLE DEVILS DON'T HAVE BEARDS
50. PURPLE DEVILS HAVE NATURAL HAIR COLORS

I shook my head. "Well I'll be da— aaaah. Well, I'll be danged. It's really in there."

"I want to make one thing very clear," Mrs. Pinson said. "We like to have a collegial learning environment at Houma-hatchee High, but that's dependent on everybody following the rules. There's zero tolerance for disrespecting the rules."

Reagan Royall sniffed. "What does 'collegial' mean exactly? Does that mean this is like college?"

Mrs. Pinson: "Purple Devils look up words they don't know."

I nodded and showed Reagan the code. "That's for real. It's Rule Number Four."

"So," Mrs. Pinson said. "Am I correct that you were sleeping in the classroom just now?"

"Yeah, but I have a disability," Reagan said, smacking her lips. "It's my ADD medication. It makes me *zleepy*."

What an amazing lie. You just knew she was faking, but she seemed so calm. Wow.

"You have attention deficit disorder?" Mrs. Pinson demanded.

"Yeah," Reagan said.

"So, you have an IEP then?" Pinson asked.

Reagan looked blank. She looked at Pinson, then at me. I mouthed the word "Yes."

An IEP is an "individualized education plan." The teachers write one up for you if you have a learning disability or are gifted or whatever. I have one, but Taleesa won't let me read it.

"Yes," Reagan said firmly. "Yes, in fact I do have an IEP."

"And what sort of medication are you taking?"

Reagan looked blank again.

"Ritalin," I whispered. Too loud, as it turns out.

"That's it," Pinson said. "I won't have lying and deception in this classroom. To the office with both of you."

"So, you're that crazy alligator lawyer girl," Reagan said as we sat in the office, awaiting our turn with the principal. "You're a colonel."

"I'm *not* a colonel," I said. "That's all a bunch of fake stuff the governor came up with."

"You know, this is weird," she said. "But I think Governor King is kind of hot. I'd like to tie him up and put some guyliner on him."

I snorted again. This girl would say anything for a laugh.

"You know, this is perfect," Reagan continued. "We'd make a good team. You're a lawyer. And I'm an outlaw. We're natural allies."

"I don't think you understand how this lawyer thing works," I said.

"Sure I do," she said. "Outlaws do what their heart tells

them. And lawyers clean up the messes. Lawyers defend you even though they know you're guilty. They're natural friends of the outlaw."

"I'm a defender of animals," I said. "All my clients are innocent."

"Not anymore," Reagan said. "I'm your client now."

"How does a girl like you get a name like Reagan? That's not a very punk name," I said.

"Are you kidding me? Ronald Reagan almost blew up the world. He believed you should pretend to be a madman so you can win in negotiations. He's absolutely punk," she said. "Actually, if you must know, my dad's a Reagan-worshipper. A big conservative. He's all about the Second Amendment and the deficit and all that. He owns like a hundred guns, they're all over the house."

"Your mom must love that," I said.

A darker chuckle from Reagan, now.

"I don't have a mom," she said. "She offed herself. Seriously, she got addicted to painkillers and committed suicide. Years ago."

For the first time, I got the feeling Reagan Royall was telling me the truth.

"My mom, too," I said. "I mean I have a stepmom now who I call my mom. But my first mom . . . it wasn't drugs. She was just depressed, I guess. She killed herself, and I can hardly even remember her."

Reagan looked at me like she was ready to throw a punch. "You had better not be scamming me," she said. "It's one thing to pretend to have ADD. It's another thing to like about this. That would be cruel."

"I'm totally not scamming you," I said.

We sat in silence for a long time. I didn't look at Reagan, she didn't look at me. Then she reached over and grabbed my hand, with a light needy pressure, the way Martinez used to do when something scary was on TV.

Just then, the principal stepped out of her office. She put her fists on her hips and looked at down at us, hand in hand, with a weary look.

"Great, and purple hair, too," she said. "All right. Into my office."

The principal's name was Rhonda St. Stephens. I didn't know much about the school, but I knew about her, because I saw a profile of her in the *Herald*. It seems that she'd read about me in the paper, too.

"Let's settle one thing now, Colonel Peale," the principal said as she sat down at her desk. "You may have friends in high places, but that's no reason to be high-handed with anyone. You were rude and dismissive to Dr. Dalton this morning. I won't have it."

At first I was angry. I never asked *anybody* to call me colonel, and now it was like a big sign around my neck. But then I went into lawyer mode. What would you say to a judge who dressed you down like this?

"I'm sorry," I said. "I really am. I didn't intend to be rude, and I didn't feel any disrespect inside, but that doesn't matter." I fished in my pocket and pulled out one of Dr. Dalton's little forms, the 341. I offered it to Mrs. St. Stephens.

"Oh, those stupid forms," the principal said. "Put it away, or give it to him yourself. Okay. I want to make one other thing straight. Miss Royall, Miss Peale. I don't know what kind of relationship the two of you have, and it's none of my business. What your parents allow is between you and them. But public display of affection is prohibited at this school. Whether you have a boyfriend or a girlfriend is none of my business, but you won't hold hands or hug or kiss anybody in this building."

Reagan and I looked at each other and burst out laughing.

"Respect," warned Ms. St. Stephens. "You treat everyone in this building with respect."

"My apologies," I said. "But I do have a question. If we're just friends, holding hands in the way girls who are friends do, is that okay?"

The principal looked back and forth between us, with a deer-in-headlights look. "Yes," she said. "I guess that's okay."

"Not that we would ever do that kind of girly-girl crap," Reagan said. "Talking about our emotions and holding hands and writing with glitter pens."

"What are you talking about?" I said. "We were just—"

"Shut *up*," Reagan said. "You are so not punk."

"Now on to the real business," Mrs. St. Stephens said. "Purple hair is prohibited in the Code of Conduct. I know you didn't read the Code of Conduct, but you should have. Or your parents should have. So I'm sending you home until the hair gets corrected."

Reagan looked stunned. And suddenly I saw something, right over the principal's shoulder, that gave me a brilliant idea.

"With all due respect, Ms. St. Stephens, given the vagueness of the purple hair rule, wouldn't it be best to go a little easier on my cli— I mean, on Reagan?"

"The rule isn't vague," the principal said. "Purple Devils have natural hair colors. It's part of the code we all live by."

"I'll concede that my friend and I were remiss in not reading the Code," I said. "And ignorance is no excuse for breaking the law. But what is the rule, exactly? What is a natural hair color?"

"Purple is not a natural hair color," Ms. St. Stephens said. "That's self-evident."

"But the rule is directed at 'purple devils,'" I said. "What's natural for a human might not be natural for a purple devil."

"I see what you're doing here, Miss Peale," the principal said. "Hairsplitting legal arguments won't get you out of this. Anyway, we've thought of that already. You'll notice that the mascot on the school emblem, even though he's a purple devil, has black hair, in a crew-cut that is a natural look for a boy."

"But in the picture on the desk, right behind you, there's a purple devil with purple hair," I said.

She turned and looked. There was indeed a photo of a high school boy, in purple body paint and little horns, posing with the school's cheerleaders. He was shirtless and wore brown rodeo chaps that I guess were supposed to look like furry devil-legs. He carried a real pitchfork, spray-painted yellow, with a deflated football impaled on it. And his hair was purple.

"That's our mascot," the principal said. "He's in a costume. It's not the same as showing up to school with purple hair. You have to use some common sense."

"I'm trying," I said. "But you've got to admit it's confusing that the rule is phrased in the 'purple devils' form. Particularly when we have competing images of a purple devil."

Ms. St. Stephens shook her head. "You're not getting her out of this."

"Here's what I propose," I said. "I'm not contesting the rule itself, I just think it's not fair to punish someone with a suspension because of an unclear rule. So what if Reagan stays at school today, without being sent home, with a promise to get rid of the purple hair by tomorrow?"

"Hey," Reagan said indignantly.

"Let me do the talking here," I said. "And to be clear, if she wants to dye her hair all black, that's a natural hair color?"

"It's a deal," the principal said. "All black, tomorrow. Now on to what I consider the much more significant issue: lying to a teacher. That's absolutely unacceptable here or in any area of life. I don't think I even have to tell you why."

I nodded. Reagan slumped in her chair and glared at both of us, still mad about the hair.

"Reagan, you lied about having an IEP," the principal said. "You didn't even know what an IEP was, did you? And Atty, you supplied her with information. You helped her lie."

Reagan kept on slumping, but somehow more defiantly than before. I sat silent for a few seconds. What could I say that wouldn't incriminate me?

Then I realized, maybe there was one thing.

"Does Reagan in fact have an IEP?" I asked. Just because she didn't have ADD didn't mean she didn't have something that sent her to, say, the school psychologist.

"Well, let's just check," the principal said, swiveling over to her computer. She typed a few things, then she turned red-faced.

"So she does have an IEP?" I asked.

"Under student privacy laws, I'm not allowed to discuss that with anyone but Reagan and her parents," Ms. St. Stephens said. "We're done here. Reagan, black hair tomorrow. You're free to go."

It wasn't until lunch that I felt the tug of the animal shelter.

"I should be cleaning the dogs' cages right now," I said, looking down at the ham sandwich on my Styrofoam plate. "I should be walking Millie and Mason and all the new dogs. School is getting me so far behind in my real life, I'll never catch up."

Reagan chewed quietly. Then: "So, you're really serious about this animal stuff, huh?"

It was lunch and we were still together, like friends who've known each other for years. Turns out we scheduled for a lot of the same stuff, even Gifted English at the end of the day. Once you've got someone to sit with at lunch, one of the scariest tasks of seventh grade is complete.

"You know," I said. "I love puppies, but I really don't think I'm any more a dog lover than most people. I just feel like everybody deserves to have a voice, and animals don't get a voice unless we help them. So that's . . . I guess I feel like that's my job in the world." I sat up a little straighter as I thought more about it. "You know, that's it. I have a job already. And all of this school stuff is just getting in the way of me doing my job."

"Sad," Reagan said. "I see this all as job training. It's getting me ready for my future career as a rebel leader in a dystopian future."

I snorted, then straightened up when I realized she was at least half-serious.

"You know," I said. "I could really see Reagan out there with a bow and arrow, fighting the dictator's robot army. So there's something we have in common. We both love science fiction."

Reagan shook her head.

"It's not science fiction," she said. "Look around you. They're already sorting us out into professions now. There's the boys in camouflage over at that table, and over at that table is your buddy Peyton, being held hostage by the other pretty-pretty girls. And over there is your crowd, the Genius Bowl types. "

"I'm not sure that's my crowd." I said. Then I squinted closer. "Hey, I see Premsyl, but I don't see Braces Girl. I wonder where she went?" I took a big bite of ham sandwich and leaned in to watch.

"Braces Girl?" Reagan asked. "You mean the chick with a camera who's right behind you?"

I turned, mouth full of ham sandwich, and was blinded by a flash. It was indeed Braces Girl, with a camera with a big fat lens like the ones they use at the Houmahatchee *Herald*.

"Now that's journalism," said Braces Girl. "Animal Advocate Eats Ham Sandwich. Do you mind telling us, Colonel Peale, why you defend alligators but eat pigs? Isn't that a contradiction?"

I couldn't say anything. I was still chewing on the ham.

"I should introduce myself," Braces Girl said. "Rebecca Braxton, cub reporter for the *Purple Devil Times*, the school's newspaper."

I swallowed.

"Braxton," I said. "So you're related to the Braxtons from the Houmahatchee *Herald*?"

"My parents," she said. She pulled out a notebook. "So, I'm wondering if you'd like to talk a little bit about eating meat. Isn't it a contradiction, for someone who loves animals, to eat ham? Where do you draw the line between an animal you help and an animal you eat?"

I was stunned. It wasn't just the question, it was all the stuff swirling around it. Premsyl, who I didn't even care about, and our encounter at the locker, and the sudden flash in my face.

"I've never really thought much about it," I said. And it was true. That stunned me, too. All the little piggies I'd been eating all this time.

"Do you have any rules about the meat you eat? Do you limit yourself to free-range meat or something?"

I blanked. And then the bell rang.

"We can catch up on this later," Rebecca Braxton said. "Think about it."

"I . . . gee, I will."

Reagan scooped up her books.

"Well, I don't know what that's about," she said. "But it wasn't about journalism and it wasn't about meat. She thinks you've got your hooks in Mr. Czech Republic. She sees you as a threat."

"But I *told* her," I said. "I told both of them I'm no threat at all."

"Welcome to high school," Reagan said. "This is what it's going to be like. A six-year battle for survival. See, they're pitting us in death matches against each other already. The dystopian future."

"So how was it?" Taleesa said when I got in the car.

"Weird," I said, suddenly relieved to be back on home turf again. Taleesa with a pen behind her ear, checking her phone for calls from editors while driving. Martinez in the back with his video game open and a peaceful look on his face, like a baby who just got his bottle.

"Everybody called me 'Colonel,'" I said. "I'm going to be in the student newspaper with a mouth full of ham sandwich. There are like three pages of written rules for how to do everything, and a lot more unwritten rules. It's a case I can't win."

"Hm," said Taleesa. "Make any new friends?"

"Just one," I said. "A girl named after Ronald Reagan."

Martinez laughed. "A girl named Ronald? Cool! I hope she has frizzy red hair and giant clown feet."

"Any cute boys?" Taleesa asked, nudging me a little with her elbow and winking.

I shrugged. "Boys aren't cute, really," I said. "Not boys my age. Premsyl was there. He's kinda cute, but if I talk to him at all, his current girlfriend will stab me."

"Can we go to McDonald's?" Martinez asked.

"This too shall pass," Taleesa said. "Junior high is tough on everybody. It'll be over before you know it."

"Six more years," I said. "I was doing fine before all this started. Can't I just homeschool and work at the animal shelter?"

"You know I don't have time for homeschooling and my work, too. I've already spent ninety minutes picking y'all up. Why on earth do they schedule the end of elementary school an hour before the end of high school? And yes, Martinez, we'll go to McDonald's before I drop you at the animal shelter."

"I love it," Martinez said. "The dogs love me when I smell like hamburger."

Sigh. "I think I'll just get one of those salads," I said. "Taleesa, was seventh grade like this for you? Was it lonely?"

Taleesa laughed. "Oh, no," she said. And then she got serious. "When I was in seventh grade, that was back before Old Martinez stopped drinking. He got arrested on some stupid charge, loitering and intoxication or something, and he lost his job. And his girlfriend at the time, she wasn't mean to me, but she just seemed to hate having me around while her man was in jail. So I liked school in the seventh grade. There was a good lunch, and people would talk to me. I got on the school paper so I wouldn't have to go home."

Well, now I felt like a total wimp.

"I'm just telling it like it is," Taleesa continued. "I know life in this town can be rough in other ways."

And then I just blurted it out. The thing we don't talk about. I couldn't stop myself.

"This town—that school—they bullied my mom to death," I said. "Didn't they? This is where it started. This is where they branded her a weirdo and never let her live it down."

Taleesa shook her head.

"I just don't know," she said. "I didn't know your mom. I don't know what she went through. I know it's the right thing to try and walk a mile in the other person's shoes, but sometimes you've just got to show some respect and say you'll never ever know what those shoes feel like. . . . Look, is there something you need to tell me? Are you being bullied or something?"

"No," I said. But as I said it, I thought of Princess P. I reached into the glove compartment for my phone. A whole day of messages.

Princess_P: Enjoy your first day at school, Colonel. Your powerful "friends" can't save you from being ridiculed at school, fatso.

Princess_P: If I were as ugly as you, I'd kill myself rather than endure high school.

Princess_P: Ever notice how a dead gator looks like it's sleeping peacefully? No, I haven't either.

ShelterMegg: Atty, see me as soon as you can. Easy has escaped from his pen.

ShelterMegg: I've informed the judge that Easy's escaped. You've got to help me find him.

ShelterMegg: We've got a court order from the judge. Meet us at the courthouse at 4 if you can.

"So much for McDonald's," I said. "We need to get to the courthouse right now."

13

HELL IS OTHER PEOPLE

Judge Grover's secretary, a woman I'd never met, looked up from her computer and smiled as if she knew me.

"Colonel Peale," she said. "The judge is waiting for you."

I stuck out my hand. "*Miss* Atticus Peale," I said. "Good to meet you."

She shook my hand, leaned in to whisper: "Go right in. He hates waiting for anybody."

I pushed open the big wooden door. Most of the Strudwick County Courthouse looks like a public restroom, with green tiles on the walls. The judge's chamber was altogether different: Big wooden bookcases, deep brown carpet, a giant oak desk and leather chairs. Judge Grover was leaning back behind the desk, looking actually kind of handsome in a three-piece suit instead of a robe. Miss Megg was there, in her shelter uniform, sitting with her hands folded in her lap like a kid being scolded by the principal.

"Good to see you, Colonel," Grover said. "Where's young Admiral Peale? Your brother's a party in all this, isn't he?"

"He couldn't make it, Your Honor," I said. Taleesa had dropped me off at the courthouse, then she and Martinez went to McDonald's. He'd be bummed that he missed someone actually using his title. I turned to Megg.

"What happened? How did Easy get loose?"

Megg shook her head. "I couldn't believe it. I went to the cage where I kept him, and he was gone. I guess he just dug and clawed, dug and clawed, until he pulled one of the boards at the corner loose. Once he got a little gap between the board and the chicken wire, he must have just squeezed through. There was blood and fur everywhere."

"That's a determined dog," I said.

"That's a dangerous dog," said Judge Grover. "I know the danger of rabies has passed. But we still have a dog on the loose that may be willing to bite someone. You took on the responsibility of keeping him out of circulation. That didn't work, so now I'm ordering that the dog, once found, will be destroyed."

That evil word again, "destroyed." I felt sick. Judge Grover pushed a paper across his desk at me.

"Here's my order," he said. "Atty, you're not a county employee, and I can't really order you to do anything. But I'm ordering Miz Megg to put forth a good-faith effort to find this dog so it can be destroyed. I want an honest search for this animal. When I walk the streets of Houmahatchee, I want to see signs that warn me about this dog and tell me who to call if I spot it. My order allows Miss Megg to delegate this work to a volunteer. I don't think I have to tell you who that volunteer should be."

I took the paper. "Understood, Your Honor," I said.

"Report back to me on your progress every week until the dog is found," Grover said. "That's all."

Megg rose to leave. I sat staring at the wood grain on Judge Grover's desk. How could I have fallen so far behind in such a short time? School had already taken me away from the shelter for most of the day. Now I was going to spend my shelter time trying to kill my favorite dog. I sighed.

"Miss Peale, are you all right?" asked the judge.

I shook it off. "Sorry, Your Honor," I said. "Yes, we'll get right on it."

And we did. I drafted a flyer on my phone, e-mailed it and a photo of Easy to the judge's secretary, and by the time we walked out of the courthouse, we had one hundred flyers in hand, fifty for me and fifty for Martinez. The court clerk loaned us two staple guns. We had thirty minutes to put up as many flyers as we could in downtown Houmahatchee before the courthouse closed and the staplers were due back. It was a start.

"I'm not doing it," Martinez said. "You've got to be crazy. I'm not going to help people kill Easy."

"It's our responsibility," I said. "We filed the suit, now we have to follow through."

"He can put me in jail if he wants," Martinez said. "Civil disobedience."

"You know, he asked me where Admiral Peale was," I said. "He respects your rank. You should respect his."

"He can kiss my entire behind," Martinez said.

Megg intervened. "Atty and I will handle this," she said to Taleesa. "I'll drop her off at your house when we're done."

So we wandered around the town square and the streets nearby, stapling up our new flyer next to the pink LOSE WEIGHT WITH TURNIP GREENS and PAYDAY LOANS EASY flyers. After the first, I stepped back to look at my work.

DANGEROUS DOG
KNOWN TO BITE
IF YOU SEE THIS ANIMAL
CONTACT STRUDWICK COUNTY
SHERIFF'S OFFICE
DO NOT FEED OR TOUCH!!

"One step forward, two steps back," Megg said. "I know it's a bummer, Atty. But I've been in this work for years. And before that, the Navy. A woman in the military. In all the work I've done, it's always one step forward, two steps back. But over time, somehow, you look back and see that you really have moved forward."

I didn't know what to say. This stapler in my hand, it felt so heavy all of a sudden. Another sigh.

"Megg," I said. "Promise me that when we find him, you'll let me be there when you put him down. I owe him that."

"I promise," Megg said. "If it's in my power to do it, I will. Though I think we have to brace ourselves for the idea that the deputies will shoot him on sight."

If you don't know anything else about the book *Gulliver's Travels*, you know that one image. A guy in old-fashioned clothes, with lace sleeves and buckles on his shoes, lying on a beach, tied down with a hundred tiny ropes. Little men—Lilliputians—lashing Gulliver down even though he's a giant compared to them.

That's how I felt when the alarm clock went off the next morning. I felt like I'd grown into some big, ugly giant, too weak to move my own limbs. And a hundred tiny cords, weak as dental floss, were holding me down. Princess P held one cord. Judge Grover held another. Braces Girl held one. And I was also tied down by all the undone work I'd left at the shelter. My column for the paper was due this evening, and I hadn't even started it.

I was too busy trying to kill my favorite dog.

Bing, went the cell phone. *Bing. Bing.* Princess P was at it again.

At the breakfast table, I felt like I was still half asleep. Martinez rambled on about how John Wednesday Addams was a former president of the United States. Dad responded in his usual too-nice way, like a teacher: "Are you *sure* about that? I'm not so sure that's correct." I think everybody—Dad serving breakfast, Martinez at the table, Taleesa rushing back and forth to get ready for an interview—were all expecting me to challenge Martinez. I just didn't feel like it. I didn't feel awake.

"Are you not hungry?" Dad said, looking at the bacon left on my plate.

"I'm not hungry for bacon," I said. "I haven't said anything until now, but I'm thinking of becoming a vegetarian."

Martinez reached over and forked the bacon off my plate. "You gotta eat meat," he said. "If you don't, you'll get mad cow disease."

Normally I would have said you've got mad cow disease all wrong, dummy. For some reason, I could only roll my eyes and sigh.

"You won't get mad cow disease," Taleesa said, passing through. "I've been a vegetarian three times. Three. And I felt great. I've been on every diet in the world, tried every food fad. Vegetarian is the best."

Martinez: "So why'd you quit, then?"

"There are things that go on between a woman and flatiron steak that sort of make everything else seem unimportant," Taleesa said. Then she turned to me. "So this is a moral thing? Right? You think it's not right to eat animals."

I shrugged. "I don't know," I said. "I know that I don't know whether it's right or wrong. And until I figure it out, I feel like I shouldn't eat any animals. And, you know, I feel like a hypocrite. I'll defend an alligator but eat a chicken. So I'm quitting. Yes, yep, that's it. I'm a vegetarian."

"You won't last," Martinez teased. "Look at the bacon, yummy bacon. Mmmm bacon, don't you want some?"

For the first time this morning I felt awake. I stood up and stared down my brother, bacon and all. "What I *want* to eat doesn't matter. I've made a decision."

"If that's how you feel," Taleesa said, "then I bet this will last a while. Looks like it's tofu stir-fry for dinner tonight."

Princess_P: Looks like your hunting down you're dog and will kill it. Best of luck to you.

Princess_P: Yeah, I know I did your/you're wrong. You hate that don't you? Good.

Princess_P: Have you ever thought of killing yourself as well? That would be nice. After the dog is gone.

I put away the phone as we pulled up to the elementary school. A sudden idea flashed through my mind.

"Martinez," I said. "If you're the one who's been texting me about Easy this morning, I'm gonna clean your clock."

Martinez hoisted his backpack and opened the car door. "What are you even talking about? Why would I text you when you're sitting right there? Bye, Dad. Bye, nutcase."

So then it was just me and Dad on the way to the high school. Something felt creepy. Dad always gets singsong pleasant when he wants to talk about something difficult.

"Atty, is everything okay at school?" he asked.

"Dad," I said. "They hold me captive there seven hours a day. One person gets to talk in the classroom, and everybody else has to raise their hands and ask permission to talk. Every minute I sit there filling in bubbles is a minute I'm not doing my real work. School itself is not okay."

"But I mean, it is abnormally bad? Are you being bullied or anything?"

"Let's see: one person gets to talk in the classroom, and everybody else has to raise their hands. Sounds like bullying to me. And all this useless stuff about x minus six equals whatever. When am I going to use that?"

"They just want you to be a well-rounded person," Dad said.

"I don't want to be well-rounded," I said. "I want to get on with my work."

"Fine," Dad said. "I think you know where I'm going,

Atty. You don't seem like yourself. I'm worried, and I think you know why I worry. And I just want you to know that if you ever need to talk about something, you can call me anytime."

"Except when you're in court, because there aren't cell phones in the courthouse," I said.

"Promise me you'll talk to somebody. If you ever feel really bad. Promise me you'll talk to someone if you feel like hurting yourself," he said.

"Dad." I sounded aggravated at first. Then I thought a little bit, reached out to touch his free hand. "Dad, let me assure you, I'm not thinking about hurting myself. I'm just sad. I'm sad about my work, and I'm sad about your work. I'm going to have to help kill Easy. I didn't save the Swamp Monster. And Jethro Gersham is going to go to prison for a murder he didn't commit. I just feel like we've been spinning our wheels all this time."

Silence from Dad.

So I went on: "This is where you're supposed to tell me that we're winning a moral victory. That it's important to go on even when you know you're going to lose. That we're heroes even if we don't save anybody, because we tried."

Dad shook his head.

"I'm not going to say that," he said. "Losing sucks. And it's not about us and our feelings and the lessons we learn. It's about Jethro and Easy and the alligator."

He was quiet again for a very long time. Then: "When you're doing what you're meant to do in this world, it can take a long time to see a result. Maybe you never will. Some people decide they just can't go on. I can't judge them. But

I know that it hurts people, it hurts the world when you decide you can't go on. Promise me you won't hurt the world, Atty."

Great. We're pulling up to the school, and suddenly I'm crying.

"I won't hurt you Dad," I said. "I promise."

I wiped my eyes and got out of the car. And then I burst into laughter. Because there, standing in front of me, was Reagan Royall.

There was no pink streak, and her hair was dyed black. But that wasn't all.

She was wearing a dress. A business-lady dress, and not one from this century. Shoulder pads that made her shoulders almost pointy. Thin white pinstripes on a charcoal-black jacket and matching skirt that went down to her ankles.

"If they're going to make me dress like an old lady, I'm going all the way," she said. "Voilà, Miss 1985. I'm going to knock the principal right in the chin with my severe shoulder pads. I've even brought some reading material."

She handed me an old, dog-eared magazine, with lots of yellow and hot pink on the cover. Also, photos of guys with bouffant hair and sunglasses, in suit jackets in all kinds of bright colors, no ties.

"Tiger Beat, May 1984 issue," she said. "It's all the rockers that were hot back then. Look, here's Simon Le Bon from Duran Duran, isn't he dreamy? And Boy George. People say he's gay, but he's denying it."

I laughed again. "What on earth are you doing with all this?"

"I'm following the rules," she said. "I'm going to do all the things Purple Devils do. And I'm going to do them in

the most annoying way possible. You can obey the letter of
the law and still defy the law. You of all people should know
that, lawyer girl."

Here's what I love most about Reagan: she does these crazy
things and gets true respect from everybody. A big beefy senior
in boots tipped an imaginary hat at her and called her ma'am,
with a flirty glint in his eye. A cheerleader in the hallway told
her earnestly that she loved the dress, and thought it was bold.

"You realize it's a joke," Reagan said.

"I know," the cheerleader said. "It's still a good look."

Teachers didn't say a word about it, but all of them seemed
to sort of fume at Reagan all day. And to make it worse,
Reagan stayed awake through every class, raising her hand
to answer. The ultimate form of sarcasm: no sarcasm at all.

I wasn't feeling so ironic, not after the encounter with
Dad. At lunch, I told Reagan the whole story.

"Does your Dad ever do that stuff to you?" I asked. "Ask
if you're thinking about hurting yourself?"

"Of course he does," she said. "I mean, I had purple hair
yesterday. I'm cross-stitching a sampler that says 'Hell is other
people.' And I spend my free time playing sad songs on the
cello. So yeah, I have like eleven of the ten signs of depression."

"What, you play cello?" I asked.

"Every day," she said. "Four hours on Saturday and
Sunday. I can also speak pretty good German. Let's just say
I went to an unusual preschool. Me and three other kids
sawing away in an Austrian immigrant's basement."

"You're blowing my mind," I said.

"I'm large," Reagan said. "I contain multitudes."

"Wow, that's deep," I said.

"It's not my line," she said. "It's from some poet. My mom used to say it when she was feeling manic or whatever. That's the kind of depression she had. Sometimes she was down, but when she was up she would talk a mile a minute and felt like she could do anything. I think that's the stuff that really worries my dad. If I play a long cello piece without messing up I'm like 'I'm king of the world!' And he looks at me all warily, like I'm turning into her."

"Lord," I said. "You ought to be able to have ups and downs without worrying that you have depression."

"Ups *and downs*, Atty," she said. "You need to stop moping about killing this dog and just go kill the dog."

We worked out a plan. First we'd go on foot, up and down the streets of Houmahatchee, putting up flyers at the intersections we couldn't reach the first day. Then we'd go outward in a kind of spiral, to the little towns like Snoad and Parrott, and flyer the convenience stores. And we'd wait for calls. The flyer said to call the sheriff's office, but I scribbled my own cell number below it on some of the flyers. Taleesa would have killed me for that, but I wanted to be in the loop if Easy was found.

"Where would I go, if I was a dog?" Martinez asked one afternoon. He showed me a list he'd been keeping crumpled in his pocket. It made me cry.

WHERE I'D GO

DOG FOOD FACTORY
ANIMAL SHELTER
MARTINEZ'S HOUSE
WHEREVER I LIVED BEFORE

"Strudwick County just isn't a good place to be a dog," Martinez said. "Maybe he split."

That's the thing. I wasn't just worried about Easy being spotted and killed. There was also the idea of Easy out there trying to make it on his own. When stray dogs came to us at the shelter, they often looked like doggy zombies, with scars and red watery eyes and scuffled fur. It was tough to think of Easy out there, scrounging in the trash for food, fighting with other dogs. Where did he sleep? I know the stars are beautiful, but I've always felt like nighttime was probably the saddest and scariest time for a stray of any sort, dog or human.

"On the bright side, at least there's not a big alligator out there to eat him," Reagan joked one day. "Too soon? Sorry."

She always pretended to be hard-hearted, but I knew that deep down inside she was rooting for Easy to get away. Easy was an outlaw, in her book. I kept hoping I could use that, in some way, to get her to join me in my shelter work.

Maybe I just wanted to spend more time with her. All the other girls seemed to be pairing up for after-school get-togethers, sleepovers where they'd do each other's hair and talk about boys they liked. I really couldn't imagine Reagan going through my closet and judging my clothes, and we rarely talked about real, actual boys—just Elric of Melnibone and Neville Longbottom and other boys from books and movies. But still, she was my best friend, and I wanted to hang out with her after school. The problem was that we both had jobs, of a sort.

"You should come home with me," Reagan said. "After I do cello practice, we could shoot clays with my dad. Or write some fanfic. I want to do a complete gender-reversed Harry Potter."

"I'm not going to sit there and watch you play cello for two hours," I said. "You should skip a day of cello and come with me to the shelter. I can't leave my shelter work."

"Well, I can't skip practice," Reagan said. "If you skip one practice, you'll skip again and again, and soon you're not a cello player at all."

"That's weird," I said. "You said that with a German accent."

"Well, I mean it," she said.

"Come on," I said. "You can come to my house after the shelter. You'll like my house. It's exactly a hundred years old, and it's creaky and creepy. Ghosts ring the doorbell in the summer, and the hallway closet pops open when you walk by."

Within days, she'd given up. She came to school on Friday with an overnight bag and a note from her dad. Even with the note, we had to haggle with the teacher in the pickup line when Reagan tried to hop into the car with me. Probably because Reagan just handed off the note to the teacher, said "keep the change!" and dashed for the car so she could get the front seat. I got in the back, and Taleesa had to get out and explain the sleepover thing to the teacher while a bunch of aggravated parents gunned their engines behind us.

"For a minute there, I thought I had jumped into the wrong car," she said. "It's cool that your brother and stepmom are black."

That irked me a bit. "Well, I told you all about that already."

"Hello, white people," Martinez said. "I'm *right here*. Should you really talk about black people like I'm not *right here*?"

It was the first time I've seen Reagan at a loss for words.

"Well, I'm just saying," she said. "You guys are, like *so* not Strudwick County."

"Born and raised here, my whole dang life," Martinez said, as if he were some old man. That wasn't actually true: He was born in Atlanta, and I was born in Florida because there's no hospital in Strudwick County. But I let it go.

"I just meant," Reagan said. "I mean, I didn't mean anything . . ."

"It's okay to talk about race, Reagan," I said. "We're not going to break into little pieces or anything. Though I guess hair, hair can be a touchy subject."

Just then, Taleesa popped back into the car.

"Hey," she said. "I'm the mom, and I guess you're Reagan. Oooh, your hair is so pretty. Atty told me about the pink stripe. I think the all-black looks really good though."

Reagan just smiled and nodded and we drove on. After a minute or so, Martinez piped up: "Mom, it's cool that you're black."

Taleesa didn't miss a beat. "Damn straight," she said.

Reagan slid down a little in the seat.

Just then, the phone rang.

"Hello?"

"Umm . . . the sheriff's department? Is this the sheriff's department?" a woman's voice said.

Oh no. Someone had spotted Easy.

"This isn't the sheriff's office," I said. "Have you seen the dog? Where?"

"It's in the woods at the end of Galvez Road, where it meets St. Stephens Highway. I live across the street. I'm not going to let my grandbabies out until it's gone. Are you the one that's going to shoot it? You sound like a little girl."

"I'll be there soon," I said. "When you hang up with me, you need to call the other number on the flyer. That's the sheriff's office."

I told Taleesa about the call, and she turned toward Galvez Road. Then I called Megg at the shelter. And I called the sheriff's office, just to make sure they got the message.

On the way, everybody was quiet except Reagan.

"What are we doing?" she asked. "Why are we going there to watch somebody shoot your dog? Why don't we just let the deputies handle it?"

"You've got a good point," Taleesa said. "I didn't even think about it. As a reporter, when I hear something's happening, I want to go see it happen. It's an instinct."

"We have a duty to see what happens," I said. "I can't explain it, exactly. Megg is there when they put the dogs to sleep. Maybe they don't even know what's going on, or why she's there, but it matters. And it matters for us to be there, too."

Martinez put down his video game and looked around in shock. "They *put doggies to sleep* right there at the shelter? Miz Megg does it?"

I sighed. "Martinez, have you paid attention to anything that's happened in the past few months? Megg and I talked about this right in front of you. We had a whole big fight about it."

"I thought they took them to a farm and did it there. A farm upstate." Martinez sounded like he was about to cry.

"I don't think Alabama even has an upstate," Reagan said. "What difference does it make?"

"It just *does* make a difference," Martinez said. My brother's voice suddenly got very small, as if he were a first-grader in bed with a fever. "I don't like this. I don't wanna go. Let's don't go there."

"We have to go," I said. "We know what Easy looks like. What if she's got the wrong dog? Do you want another dog to die because of mistaken identity?"

And then we were there. The end of Galvez Road, just past the edge of town. On one side, a single-wide trailer with chain-link fence around it and a kiddie pool in the back. In the front yard, a little windmill that, when it spun in the wind, made a little wooden man chop endlessly at a piece of wood. Across the street from the trailer, a big two-story house up on the hill with a fence and a brick-and-iron gate. The driveway ran up the hill and ended in a big cobblestone circle in front of the house. I'd noticed the house before—we called it the Downton Abbey house sometimes—but until now I'd never noticed the name on the mailbox out front.

B GRADDOCH.

A woman in a nightgown was standing on the porch of the trailer. When we got out of the car, she just pointed to the woods across the field on the other side of St. Stephens Highway. "He's over there."

We all peered at the field and the woods. No dog. Dying yellow weeds in the field, and behind them, purple-brown pine tree trunks.

We were safe.

There was a crunch of gravel as a sheriff's office patrol car pulled up behind us. Out came Troy Butler, the radio on his shoulder squawking away.

"Miss Taleesa, Colonel Peale," he said nodding.

"Not a colonel," I said.

"I'll make a note of it," he said. "So y'all have found our dog?"

"I don't know," I said. "We can't see anything."

Butler looked out over the field. Then put both pinkies in his mouth and whistled. "EASY!!" he shouted.

A dog's head popped up from the weeds. Then the dog stood up and looked at us intently. There was no doubt it was Easy. Black all over his back, a white face and chest with Dalmatian freckles, the one big black dot over one eye. All of a sudden I missed Easy with a real ache. And I knew that ache was about to get worse.

"It's the one?" Butler asked.

I couldn't speak. I nodded.

"Y'all kids get in the car," Butler said. "This is a dangerous dog. I'll handle this."

Butler whistled and called Easy. Easy just stood there.

"I can't hit him from here, not with just a pistol," Butler said through the rolled-down window. "I've got to get him closer. Maybe he'll come if y'all call him."

"I ain't doing that," Martinez said.

"I've never met the dog before," Reagan said. "I don't snitch to the police."

Butler looked at me. "Atty?"

I nodded. But when I drew my breath in to call out, I started sobbing instead, like I haven't cried in years. "I'm sorry," I told him between gasps.

But Troy Butler had already moved on. He was texting on his phone. "I could hit him if I had a rifle. I bet Backsley Graddoch has one up there at his house."

I couldn't stop crying. In front of Butler and Reagan and everybody. It was embarrassing. By the time I stopped gasping, everybody was out of the car again, staring at the woods. Backsley Graddoch was there, too, looking strange in his suit, with a military-looking assault rifle cradled under his arm.

"I'll take the shot," Graddoch told Butler. "It's my rifle, I've got it sighted in. I used to shoot competitively. I was the best shot in the county."

"Fine with me," Butler said. "So here's the plan. The dog's lying down over there in the grass somewhere. We just saw him. If I call out to him, he should stick his head up. Then you plug him. I'm guessing he'll run after the first one, like a deer, so you've got one shot."

"Ready when you are." Graddoch pointed his rifle toward the field where we'd seen the dog.

Butler whistled. "EASSSYY!!" he shouted.

The freckled head popped up.

Graddoch took in a deep breath, then slowly started to exhale. I saw his finger twitch on the trigger.

"SUH-WING, BATTER!!" Reagan shouted suddenly.

A shot rang out. I don't know where it went, but it didn't hit Easy. The dog turned and ran toward the pines as fast as he could. Graddoch's rifle cracked twice more, but Easy kept going, disappearing into the woods.

"Gaaah," Graddoch said. He turned to me. "You! the judge ordered you not to interfere with catching this dog. Why did you do that?"

"It wasn't me, Mr. Graddoch, I swear," I said, turning to Reagan.

Reagan popped earphones out of her ear, looked up from her phone. "What? Sorry, I was watching the playoffs on my phone. Did I mess you up?"

It was like her attention deficit disorder lie earlier. So bold, you almost wanted to clap.

"Young lady, don't play games with me," he said. "You fouled my shot on purpose."

Reagan laughed. "Give me a break," she said. "I coulda made that shot, even with somebody yelling in my ear. And I'm just a dainty little girl."

Graddoch turned to me. "Miss Peale, this is where your meddling has got us," he said. "A dangerous dog on the loose. A deputy's time wasted, and the court's time wasted, on animals that are clearly dangerous. I hope you learn your lesson soon. These frivolous lawsuits of yours are making the world less safe for everybody."

"*Speaking* of safety," Reagan interjected. "Is your safety on now? And come to think of it, do you even know what's in those trees across the street? A responsible shooter always knows what's behind the thing he's shooting at. Any idea at all?"

Graddoch looked down at his rifle and grumbled when he realized the safety was not, in fact, on. He lifted the gun up—more or less in our direction—as he moved to switch it on. Reagan suddenly jerked me over to her side, and put a hand up like a cop stopping traffic.

"Whoa, cowboy!" she said. "Keep that weapon down-range. Deputy, are you really going to let this man swing a gun around while he yells at little girls?"

Butler patted Graddoch on the back.

"Thank you, Mr. Graddoch," he said. "Looks like we're done here. Best to clear out."

Graddoch slung the rifle over his shoulder and skulked off. "Trust me," he said. "Judge Grover will hear about this."

14

I t's hard to have a sleepover with someone who is large and contains multitudes. Reagan wasn't herself at all during her time at my house. She called Dad and Taleesa "Ma'am" and "Sir."

At the dinner table—we rarely actually sit down for a family dinner, but we always pretend when company comes—she spent most of the time quizzing Dad about how he became a lawyer, where he went to law school, and what kind of law he practiced. She really got him going, to the point that he was telling his old military stories and talking about old criminal cases.

"I'm actually working on a capital murder case now, but it's about to come to a close," he said.

Martinez and I both sat bolt upright.

"What?" I asked. "Jethro Gersham's coming to a close? I thought you said it would take more than a year to come to trial."

Dad shook his head.

"Forget I said anything," he said. "It's all between me and my client."

"No," I said. "You said it's coming to a close. That means he really is pleading guilty. How can you let him do that? Why would he do that? You know he's innocent."

"My job is to get the best outcome for my client," Dad said. "To some extent, he's the one who decides what's the best outcome. So if he was going to plead—and I'm not saying he is—I can only try to persuade him otherwise."

Martinez crossed his arms and pouted through the rest of dinner. Dad and Taleesa didn't even notice. They were so delighted with well-behaved little Reagan Royall. Later, when we were washing dishes, Dad told me he fully approved of my friendship with Reagan.

"She's delightful," he said. "What a sparkling conversationalist."

"She just sat there and let you talk, Dad," I said.

"Well, at least somebody will," he said.

I went straight to the living room to confront Reagan directly. She was sitting daintily on the couch with Taleesa.

"What is up with you, Reagan?" I said. "You haven't told a single lie or broken a single rule since you got here."

"That would be rude," Reagan said. "I'm a guest in this house. It's not like school, where I'm a captive."

Outside of school, Reagan was like an old lady, disciplined and set in her ways. She refused to drink tea or Coke after 5 p.m. She had to take her pill exactly at eight, and had to go to bed at exactly nine. Before bed she pulled a Bible out of her backpack and read.

"You can read the whole Bible in a year if you cover four chapters a day," she said. "I've read it four times since I was seven."

At bedtime, it was lights out. I lay on a futon on the floor and Reagan lay on my twin bed, staring up at the ceiling.

"Hey," I whispered. "Now we can talk. You want to talk?"

"I'm praying," she said.

I waited a few minutes. "Now can we talk?"

"Time to sleep," Reagan said.

"Good Lord," I said. "You're like a soldier of sleep. Everything has to be done just right. What's up with you?"

"Atty, there's a good chance I have a mental illness," she said. "The same one that killed my mother. This is how you manage that illness. Discipline. Faith."

I wanted to say: "Maybe you're not clear about the mental illness you really have. Maybe you're obsessive-compulsive." But I didn't say anything. What do I know? I'm a twelve-year-old girl who talks to a toy squirrel.

And you know? She was right about not drinking tea after five. A minute or two after we talked, I was fast asleep.

It might have been hours later that I woke up again, but it seemed like moments. It was dark, and I heard the sound of a scuffle.

"Get off of me, weirdo!" Reagan said.

"Ahh!" Martinez gasped.

"Wha? What's going on?" I said.

Reagan: "Your crazy brother is trying to get into bed with me."

Martinez: "I was looking for Atty! Why are you in her bed?"

Me: "She's a guest in this house, Martinez. She gets the bed, I get the floor. What is it you need, Martinez?"

My brother plopped down on the floor beside me. "I want to talk about Jethro. He's innocent, I just know it. We can't let him plead guilty."

I shook my head. "We need to stay out of it. It's not our case. We could get Dad in trouble. We probably already know more about the case than we should."

Martinez sighed. "That's not like you, Atty. Since when do you give up on somebody you know is innocent?"

In the moonlight, I could see Reagan rolling over and resting her head on her elbow. "So what is it you propose we do, kid? Ride around on our bikes, with little tassels and baskets, snooping around like amateur sleuths from some 1950s kids' book?"

Martinez, excitedly: "Yes!"

Reagan shrugged. "I'm in. Sounds pretty cool, actually."

"And we don't even need bikes," Martinez said. "We can use the hunt for Easy as an excuse and get Mom to drive us to all the key sites where we want to investigate."

"I don't know about this," I said. "I don't like lying to Taleesa. She's taking a lot of time away from her freelance work to help us."

Even now, as I tell you this, I feel terrible for even thinking about lying to Taleesa. But the fact is that within minutes, all three of us were on the floor with a flashlight, sketching out a list of the places we needed to get Taleesa to take us to do our own investigation.

PAWNSHOP
MARINA
JETHRO'S HOUSE

AMBROSE'S CHURCH
WHEREVER AMBROSE BOUGHT HIS
LOTTERY TICKET.

The thing I liked best was that Reagan was now in on our daily hunt for Easy.

I thought lying to Taleesa would be the worst part of the plan. But the worst was lying to Miss Megg.

I knew it was time to pull back on the search for Easy and spend more time at the shelter, doing my real job. One week during the search, I even missed my deadline to get the pets column in the Houmahatchee *Herald*. But I tried to put all that out of my mind and told Megg we were making one last push to get the word out and find the dog.

I think she knew something strange was up.

"Seems like you should do a really good search in the place where you saw him last, out near Backsley Graddoch's house," she said.

"Well, I'm thinking Easy probably got out of the area after being shot at," I said. "So I'm thinking we'll search in some new places. Maybe we'll even go to Florida."

"The state line is twelve miles from the last place you saw Easy," Megg said.

"Well, dogs walk fast," I said.

Megg narrowed her eyes a little, like she didn't believe me.

"You're a good kid, Atty," she said. "You're doing more than you have to do, and I know your heart's in the right place. So I'm going to trust that whatever this is that you're doing, it's the right thing."

What Megg said bothered me. But it really did feel right to pile into the car with Reagan at the end of the day, knowing I had a friend who was joining me in my work. A partner in crime.

"All right, dog hunters," Taleesa said as Reagan plopped into the front seat. "Where to this time?"

"Jethro Ger—" Martinez started, before I put a hand over his mouth.

"Over by the Speedy Queen," I said. "It's a place we haven't covered yet."

Martinez glared at me. "Don't cover my mouth like that. It's assault."

"Listen, dummy," I whispered in his ear. "The Speedy Queen's next to Jethro's house. We don't want to *tell* Taleesa we're going to Jethro's house."

It really was a place we should have put out flyers before. The Speedy Queen was a drive-in burger place where you could press on a button and order fries and a shake through a scratchy speaker, then wait for them to bring it out to you. It was always packed with old people in convertibles, moms and dads with little kids in the back seat, shirtless guys in pickups trying to flirt with the waitresses. The place was so full, we had to park across the street.

"Guess we'll need to ask the manager if we can put up flyers here," Taleesa said. "Do you want to do that, or do you want me to?"

This was our chance. "They might be more willing to listen to a grown-up," I said. "I tell you what: you go in and ask about the flyers, and we'll knock on a few doors down the street and ask people if they've seen anything."

Taleesa looked back at me with narrowed eyes. "I don't know if that's safe," she said.

"We're high schoolers now, Atty and I," Reagan said. "We'll go in a group. And look, I carry pepper spray on my key ring."

Taleesa looked back and forth to both of us. "Ten minutes. I want you back in ten minutes, tops."

Across the street from the Speedy Queen sat a row of old houses, a couple with boards on the windows and FOR SALE signs in the yard, others with windmills on the lawn and furniture on the porch. And one with grass and weeds as tall as your chin, and a sign in front. "THIS PROPERTY IS IN VIOLATION OF CITY CODE. IF YOU ARE THE OWNER, PLEASE CALL CODE ENFORCEMENT AT 251-555-9301."

"That's Jethro's house," I said. "I guess he's in trouble with the city for not cutting his grass. Hard to cut your grass when you're in jail."

"Well let's go take a look," Reagan said.

Soon we stood at the edge of Jethro's yard. It looked just like the home of someone who'd been snatched up by the police and never allowed to return. I could see the white plastic tips of little cigars sticking out of an ashtray by the porch swing. A stepladder stood open right in front of the door, next to a pan of paint with a paint-roller still in it. On the walkway up to the porch lay a lumpy, half-full garbage bag, once black but now faded to an icky gray. Reagan stepped forward and nudged the bag with her toe. A familiar rattle.

"It's full of old aluminum cans," she said. "How much Coke does this guy drink? How much beer does he drink?"

Martinez brushed right past us to the porch and tried to

peer into Jethro's windows. I followed. The paint pan on the porch was full of sky-blue paint, now dried, with the roller stuck to the pan forever.

"That's weird," I said. "The house is gray, the paint here is blue. What was he painting?"

Reagan tapped me on the shoulder, pointed upward. Most of the porch ceiling was covered in dirty, peeling white paint. About a third of it was fresh, sky blue—part of an unfinished paint job.

"Haint blue," Reagan said. "My dad's a fan of that, too. Some people say that if you paint your porch ceiling blue, it keeps bugs away. Some people say it scares away ghosts."

Martinez turned to us with a serious look. "Nobody touch anything," he said. "This is a crime scene."

I rolled my eyes. "It's exactly the opposite of that," I said. "You're just saying that because you heard it on a TV show somewhere."

Martinez shrugged. "The point is, there are clues here. We need to look out for clues."

"Doesn't seem like much to me," Reagan said. "If you really want clues, you should talk to the neighbors. I bet Gersham has an alibi for where he was at the time of the murder. Let's go knock on some doors."

We both stood silent for a moment.

"What?" Reagan said.

"Nothing," I said. "It's just weird, knocking on people's doors uninvited. I have to kind of mentally prepare myself."

"Oh, good heavens, we don't have time for that," Reagan said. "Haven't you ever had to knock on a stranger's door before? Witnessing? Girl Scout cookies? No?"

"Just give me a second," I said.

"Oh, come on," Reagan said, talking me by the arm. She strode across the yard to the neighbor's porch and then held my hand up. "Make a fist," she said. Then she proceeded to knock on the door with my hand.

A sleepy-looking old white guy answered just as I was pulling up a photo of Easy on my phone. I asked the man if he'd seen a dog like this one.

"I'm sorry, honey, I ain't seen your pet," he said. "You should try the animal shelter."

"What if we tried next door?" Reagan asked. "This guy with the long grass. Does anybody live there?"

"That's old Jethro's place," the man said. "You don't need to go over there. He ain't there, he's in jail for murder."

I tried to act surprised. "You mean Jethro Gersham? The guy who shot the pawnshop owner?"

The man nodded. "I seen it when they arrested him," he said. "It was right over there in his yard. That sack full of beer cans, he was carrying it when they came to arrest him. I guess I should have moved it, and cut his yard, but I didn't want to touch it because I guess it's a crime scene."

Martinez started poking me in the ribs, as if to say I Told You So.

"Why did he have a bag of beer cans?" Reagan asked.

"We ain't exactly rich around here," the man said. "A lot of folks collect old cans and recycle 'em for money. I do it myself when the price is up."

"So he was collecting cans on the side of the road on the day of the murder?" I asked.

"Well, I reckon he was always doing that," the man

said. "I remember that morning, I saw him on his porch, painting. I was about to weed-eat my yard and he asked me to hold off so I wouldn't get grass in his paint. Then about thirty minutes later he tells me he got a call and had to go to the pawnshop and could I hold off a little longer because he was going to finish painting when he gets back. And he has a trash bag in his hand when he says it. You know, he don't have a car so he walks everywhere. So he always had a trash bag. And then he comes back about an hour later with the bag over his shoulder and the police just seem to show up out of nowhere."

"Wow, I bet the police quizzed you all about that," I said.

"Not a bit," the man said. "Some lawyer-man came around and asked. In fact I should probably shut up about it. Maybe they'll ask me to come to court."

We thanked the man and left. The ten minutes were almost up.

"I'm impressed, Atty," Reagan said as we walked back to the Speedy Queen. "You're as good a liar as I am. 'You mean, the guy who killed the pawnshop owner?' What an actor!"

"Yeah, too bad she didn't learn anything," Martinez said.

"Oh, I think there's some evidence there," I said. "If you're carrying a lottery ticket in your pocket, why bother to collect old beer cans for money? Why stroll through town picking up beer cans when you've got a murder weapon in your pocket? If I killed a guy, I'd run straight to Red Creek and toss the gun off the bridge."

Reagan nodded. "Good stuff. But not good enough to get him out of jail. And it sounds like stuff your dad already knows."

"True," I said. "But to me, it's a good sign. It's a sign that we're right, that he didn't do it. And it's evidence we collected by ourselves. You know, I really think we can do this."

Our next stop was First Baptist Church of Red Creek, the place where Ambrose went to church. It was a complete bust. When Taleesa agreed to take us out there, I expected to walk in and start asking the pastor and the choir director a bunch of questions. Instead, the gravel parking lot was empty, the big wooden church doors closed and locked. We wound up stapling "have you seen this dog" flyers to the power poles along the street, just like we told Taleesa we would.

"I could have warned you that wouldn't work," Reagan said as we trudged down the road, staple guns in hand. "Unless a church has a day care, it's going to be closed during the workweek. You're the smartest girl I know, Atty, but you don't know a lot about church."

I laughed. "So this is the point where you start witnessing to me?"

"I might," she said. "When the time is right. I might even pray for you sometime, but not in a mean way."

"No need to pray for me," I said. "Pray for Easy. Pray for Jethro. Pray for justice. Okay, you can pray for me a little. Pray I get my homework and the *Herald* column both finished this week."

Reagan pulled a rolled-up newspaper out of the pocket of her hoodie. "That reminds me. Let's see how the column came out this week."

"Wait, where did you get that paper?" I asked.

"I slipped it out of the mailbox at that house back there," she said, thumbing through the paper. "You didn't even notice, did you? Expert shoplifting skills."

"Reagan! You beat all I've ever seen," I said. "One minute, you're preaching at me, the next minute you're stealing from people."

"How big am I?" she said, arching an eyebrow. "What do I contain? Say it."

"Large," I sighed. "Multitudes."

"Anyway, I'm just borrowing it," she said. "We're going to pass the same house on the way back and I can retu— oh wait. Oh, no. Oh, no."

"What is it?" I said, grasping for the paper.

"'Plea hearing Friday for murder suspect,'" Reagan read. "It's right here on Page 3A. It says Jethro's going to court Friday morning and is expected to enter a guilty plea."

Looking over her shoulder, I read it myself. My heart sank. How could Dad do this and not even tell us?

"This is serious, Reagan," I said. "We have to step up our investigation. We have three days."

15

B *ing.*
    Checking your phone in bed can make you temporarily blind. I read that in a newspaper article. On my phone. Probably in bed. I just can't resist. Not when someone's sending me a message.

> **Princess P:** On Friday morning, it's over for your murderer friend. You lose again.

Bing. From Princess P, a photo of the Swamp Monster, dead in the back of a pickup truck.

Who does this stuff? Why is someone so intent on making me suffer? I started to send a message back, then thought better of it.

Don't feed the trolls, Atty, I thought. *Think. Think about what we're going to do with the time we have left. Think about how we win—how Jethro Gersham wins—not how Princess P loses.*

I typed out a message. To Martinez.

Atticustpeale: What's the plan? Are you up? What's the plan?

Bing.

CinqueMartinez: We skip school and ride our bikes to the places we want to investigate. The marina. The store in Florida where he bought the lottery ticket.

I shook my head, even though I was in the dark and no one could see me.

Atticustpeale: This is real life, not a movie. We skip school, we get grounded and can't work. And maybe the cops come looking. Plus do you know how to get to the marina?

Bing.

CinqueMartinez: Jerk.

Bing.

CinqueMartinez: Well, we have Friday.

Friday was the day Jethro's plea hearing was scheduled. It was also a school holiday. I hear that up north, school systems have makeup days for snow: make it through winter without a snow day, and you get a day off anyway. In Strudwick County we have hurricane days. Make it to mid-October without school closing for a tropical storm, and you get a four-day weekend for Columbus Day. Friday, Saturday, Sunday, Columbus Day.

So that meant we'd be able to do a little investigation on the same day the plea deal came up. But the courthouse opens at 9 a.m.

Jethro could have his hearing and be on his way to prison by 9:30.

Atticustpeale: We'd have to start early. We'd have to work fast.

CinqueMartinez: Leave it to me.

The next day at breakfast, Martinez pounced. "So, we're off Friday," he said. "Can we come to the courthouse with you, Dad?"

We'd done that before: reading quietly on a bench in the back of a courtroom on our holiday. Martinez hated it. Cell phones and video games were banned from the courtroom. With a screen in front of him, he was as motionless as a sponge on the ocean floor. Without it, he couldn't sit still.

"I see what you're doing," Dad said. "Yes, Jethro's plea hearing is Friday. No, I'm not going to discuss it further. And no, you two are not going to be there to unfurl your protest banner. You're going with Taleesa. Wherever she's going."

We've also spent the October holiday with her, some years, as she interviewed cancer researchers in Auburn, covered Mobile's first (and last) Oktoberfest parade and talked to people in Cheaha State Park who were making a movie about Bigfoot.

"Actually," Taleesa said. "I was planning Friday as a writing day. Just going to stay here while you kids do your thing."

"You deserve a day off, Mom," Martinez said.

Taleesa chuckled. "I'm a freelancer. We don't get days off."

"We should go to the beach," Martinez said. "Other people go on vacations. We just watch our parents work."

Always good with the guilt, that Martinez.

"The beach in October?" Taleesa said. "The water'll be cold. There won't be anything to do."

"Oh, that's the best time," Martinez said. "Nobody else will be there. We'll have Panama City all to ourselves. We can hit the shops and walk on the beach. We don't have to go in the water."

Suddenly I realized what Martinez was doing. So I pitched in: "Maybe you could get a story out of it: Five things to do in Panama City in the off-season. Or maybe a business story about how the tourist traps survive in the winter."

Taleesa thought for a second. "The business journals do pay well. And I owe the *Herald* a feature next month. Two birds, one stone. I like it."

"Aaaand," I said, raising my voice in excitement. "Your research will consist of going to the beach and seeing what there is to do. Enjoying yourself. You can have a day off and still get something useful done."

Taleesa nodded. "I like it."

"And we can stop and buy a lottery ticket just over the state line," Martinez said.

There it was: the bass drop. Martinez was trying to get us to the shop where J. D. Ambrose bought his lottery ticket before he was murdered.

"I smell something fishy here," Dad said. "What are y'all really up to?"

Martinez was silent. I jumped in.

"You caught me, Dad," I said. " I've been wanting to put up some flyers about Easy across the Florida line. Everybody stops at that one gas station to buy lottery tickets. This is my chance."

Dad turned to Taleesa. "Sounds like fun," he said. "Wish I could go."

And we were in.

The last time Martinez woke us all up before dawn was Christmas. When he was five. So I was a little perturbed when he turned on my bedroom light that Friday morning, threw back the covers, and put a cold can of Coke in my hand.

"Time to go," he said. "You'll probably need some caffeine. You'll want to tap it a couple times before you open it."

Through my squinted eyes, I could see him already decked out in ridiculous beach garb: loud tie-dye shorts, sandals, and that too-small airbrushed shirt of a blue dolphin jumping out of the water that we bought during Spring Break like eighteen months earlier. The airbrush artists didn't even get our names right: mine said "Addy" and his was "Martin Ed," but he loved that shirt anyway.

"Jeez, what time is it?" I said.

"Five-thirty," my brother said. "We have to hurry. Dad's already up and getting ready for work."

I drifted off. In my dream, I was in an icy forest with trees with red metal apples on them, apples with droplets of water on their sides. I reached out to grab one and CLONK! woke up when the Coke fell off the bed and hit the floor.

That's when it hit me. Five-thirty. Three and a half hours to find evidence to clear Jethro Gersham. I ran to the bathroom, brushed my teeth while sitting on the toilet, and rushed so fast to get dressed I put my shoes on before my pants and had to take them off again.

"Good Lord," Taleesa said. "What is the rush? I get a day off and I can't even sleep in."

"We don't want to miss it," Martinez said, practically pulling Taleesa out of the bed.

"Miss what?" Taleesa said.

"The tide," he said. "High tide is at 9:30. We don't want to miss it."

He'd done this for a couple of days. Trying to come up with beachy-sounding reasons to get there early. On Wednesday he said we didn't want to miss the scalloping; on Thursday, we needed to go early to avoid a nor'easter. I was pretty sure he had no idea what any of those words meant.

As we hounded and nagged Taleesa, Dad was beginning to look and smell like a big court date. Lots of aftershave, a new tie. Hair slicked back so every hair was in place. Still, Taleesa resisted rushing. She made us all sit down and eat breakfast together. She took the beach bags Martinez hastily packed, dumped them out, and started loading them again. "So do we really need floaties? We're not going in the water. Sunscreen, maybe you guys can use."

It was agonizing. By the time we pulled out, Dad was

right behind us, loading his briefcase into the car. It was 8:30 a.m. Three hours packing for a one-hour drive to the beach! But then, I realized: Taleesa was the only one who really thought of this as a beach trip.

I sat in the back with Martinez, so we could conspire.

"Chill out with the high-tide stuff," I whispered. "Let me handle it from here."

"I can't help being intense," he whispered back. "We're Jethro's only hope."

"You need to brace yourself," I said. "Chances are we won't find much of anything."

"The best clues come out right at the last minute," he said. "That's how it happens in the movies."

Bing.

Princess_P: Just a few minutes and another murderer gone.

I ignored it.

Princess_P: Halloween's coming. Have you thought of going as a pig? All you need is a curly tail, you little fatty.

I was so sick of this. What could I say to hurt this person back?

I sighed and looked out the window, watching for the "Florida State Line" sign. Call me crazy, but I see a big difference between Alabama and Florida, even though it's just twelve miles away from home. Even though on both sides of the county line, it's all pine trees in rows, and swamps, and humidity and sun and gas stations that sell grody foods in red pickle jars. I guess it's the signs. In Florida, all the signs promise sun and fun down the road. In Strudwick County, the signs are all about cheap beer, Marine recruiting, and the coming end of the world. "ARE YOU READY?" they ask.

"There it is," Martinez said. "Gas and Florida lotto, next left."

"Oh, all right," Taleesa said. "When we win the Pick Six, I'm getting a hot tub. What are you getting, Atty?"

"A good air conditioner for the animal shelter," I said. "Ads in big newspapers to help us find homes for animals."

We pulled in to the store under a big sign that read STATE LINE LOTTO CENTER AND FUEL. The parking lot was all gravel, and the gas pumps were super-old, the square kind with mechanical numbers on them instead of a screen. The parking lot was nearly full, a fact I attributed to the offers made in bold pink letters on the side of the building.

WELCOME ALABAMIANS
LOTTERY
BEER ON SUNDAY
WINGS

Inside, it smelled like fried food. People milled around a counter where chicken and fries sat under a heat lamp. Bandanas and car tags and were for sale on racks, and the wall was lined with T-shirts you could buy for $13.99. One had a Confederate flag and the words COME AND TAKE IT. Another had Jesus on the cross with the inscription PAID THE COST TO BE THE BOSS.

"Clues," Martinez said. "We have just a couple of minutes to find all the clues."

He was still convinced, I think, that clues came clearly marked with pawprints, like in a kids' show. I just played along, pulling some Easy flyers out of my bag. "I'll distract them, you look," I said.

A mean-looking white lady leaned on the counter, scowling at a magazine. When she saw me, the mean look went away and she turned into a grandma. She wore a name tag that read ARLENE.

"How can I help you, sweetie?" she said.

I thrust the flyer at Arlene. "Ma'am, I don't suppose you've seen this dog?" That's how I always opened. Nobody ever says "I haven't seen him." They always say "I wish I could help you." And that's when you ask to put the flyers up.

But Arlene didn't do what I expected. She peered at the paper and smiled. "I know that dog. That's Edward."

I didn't even know what to say. "Wha? You've really seen him?"

"Oh, I seen him," Arlene said. "He used to come in every week with his owner. That guy J.D. He bought a ticket ever' week."

"J.D.," I said. "Jefferson Davis Ambrose? The pawnshop owner?"

"I reckon that's what J.D. stands for," Arlene said. "Of course he don't come in anymore. He's dead. *A black guy shot him right in his own store.*"

She said that last bit in a harsh whisper, casting a nervous glance at Taleesa as she said it. That stuff always hacks me off, but now was not the time to deal with it.

"So Ambrose brought in this dog, every week, and his name is Edward," I repeated.

"That's what I said," Arlene said. "Had a little 'E' on his dog tag. J.D. loved that dog. It was with him all the time. It was with him last time I seen him. Although J.D. wasn't playing the lottery then. He'd already won. He came back one last time to thank us. Look, he got his picture made with us."

Sure enough, on the wall was a sign that said: HOME OF A LOTTERY WINNER. Beneath it, a photo of Arlene and some other people with a guy holding a lottery ticket. And right there next to the guy with the ticket, his tongue hanging happily, was Easy.

My head was spinning. Easy was the murder victim's dog. Maybe the last living witness to the murder—except for whoever did it. Maybe clues do have pawprints on them.

"Wow," I said. "So what did y'all talk about on that last visit?"

"Well, he thanked us for being so good to him all these years, and he gave God the glory for winning the lottery, and he said he was going to use the money to cancel all the debts everybody owed him—he thought it was the Christian thing to do—and said he was going to retire out of the pawn business, " Arlene said. "Oh, and he said his brother-in-law, who was his business partner, sort of, wasn't too happy about closing the place."

"Did he say why?" I asked.

"Well, not really, but I can guess," Arlene said. "I know his brother-in-law, Gary Dudley. He comes in here ever so often to get beer on Sunday. To hear him tell it, he's a full partner in the pawnshop with J.D., but that's not what J.D. said. J.D. said he owned most of the business, but that a little bit of it belongs to his sister—Gary's wife—and J.D. keeps Gary on as an employee because he's family. J.D. didn't have a wife or kids of his own. So I guess Gary was worried about losing his job. If J.D. wanted to close the shop, there wasn't much Gary or his wife could do about it, I reckon."

Whoa. I felt queasy, though with fear or excitement I couldn't tell. I pulled out my phone and looked up "Gary Dudley." I needed a Facebook page or something. Something with a photo. Waiting . . . Waiting . . .

There. My heart stopped.

"Martinez!" I shouted. "It's Cloudy Hair. Cloudy Hair is the murderer!"

Martinez rushed up, and his eyes got wide as he looked at my phone. It was a Facebook profile photo of a man we both knew. Old, slim, mean-looking with a cloud of stringy white hair.

"It is him," Martinez said. "The guy from the animal shelter. The guy who wanted to kill Easy!"

Taleesa came up, too. I went through everything Arlene had told me.

"So, you see, Jethro really didn't do it after all," I said. "Cloudy Hair framed him."

Taleesa shook her head. "I don't follow you."

"Okay," I said. "Let's look at what we know. We know the man we know as Cloudy Hair is really Gary Dudley, the brother of the murder victim. And we know that the dog we know as Easy is really Edward, the murder victim's dog."

Taleesa nodded.

"And we know that Cloudy Hair shot Easy, and that Easy bit Cloudy Hair, and a day or so later, Cloudy Hair came to the animal shelter hoping to claim Easy. Claim him so he could shoot him. Or just have him put down."

"Strange," Taleesa said. "But not proof of murder."

"Actually, *very* strange," I said. "I mean, two days after your brother-in-law is murdered, you want to hunt down and kill his dog?"

"Maybe he tried to take Easy in, and Easy bit him, and he shot Easy, and Easy ran off," Taleesa said.

"Fine, but why keep hunting? Why not just let him go? Once he's in the pound, likely to be put to sleep, why try to claim him so you can shoot him yourself?"

Martinez lit up. "Because the dog is evidence," he said. "You shot the dog, and for all you know, there's a bullet still in the dog's body."

Taleesa: "Still don't get it."

"Okay, let's tell the story another way. I'm Gary Dudley, cloudy-haired mean guy. My boss, who is my wife's brother, wants to close his business because he won the lottery. I don't have any say in it, and I'll lose my job. But if my brother-in-law is dead, then my wife inherits the business *and the lottery ticket*. I'll be rich."

Taleesa, skeptically: "Go on."

"It just so happens that my brother-in-law has a bunch of guns in his store, all pawned by various people, and he's starting to call all the gun owners and tell them to come claim their guns. For free. And you know—because you've seen the X mark he puts on his paperwork—that one of the gun owners can't read, can't even write his name. Maybe you even talk to your brother-in-law about that to make sure you're right."

Now even Arlene was drawn in. "Keep going," she said.

"So you take Jethro's gun out of storage and you load it. You wait for a time when the shop is empty, and you use your brother-in-law's cell phone to call Jethro to come get his gun. When you're sure Jethro's on the way, you shoot your brother-in-law in the back room of the store. And you type up a nonsense receipt—"

"I knew that was a clue," Martinez shouted.

"—And you staple it to the lottery ticket. You give Jethro both. You tell him to make sure to hang on to that receipt, to prove he got the gun back fair and square. Jethro leaves with the murder weapon and the lottery ticket, thinking you've made his day. Then you just walk away. An hour or so later, a random customer walks in, wonders why no one's around, goes to the back office to find him. Dead body, police called, cell phone checked, cops go to Jethro's house. And Jethro—who calls a receipt a 'ticket'—is like, yeah, I got the gun and the ticket right here."

Taleesa nodded. "The perfect crime. Too perfect, sounds like a conspiracy theory."

"Except it's not perfect. One thing goes wrong with the plan. When you shoot your brother-in-law, his loyal dog tries to defend him, biting you on the leg. You shoot the dog, and you don't know how badly he's hurt, because he runs away. So now you're limping around with a dog bite on your leg, and maybe there's a dog out there with a bullet in it from the murder weapon. Not so good for you if someone puts the two together."

Taleesa seemed convinced now. "That's pretty compelling," she said. "Atty, you're a genius! Your dad's going to feel stupid for not finding all this before."

Martinez shook his head. "There are still some problems, though. Jethro said the guy who gave him the receipt was a guy in a red hat."

"Commonly used to cover hair, cloudy and otherwise," I said.

"And how does Easy get away, if Cloudy Hair shoots him inside the pawn shop?" Taleesa asked. "It's not like he can open doors."

"I can see y'all have never been to Ambrose's store," Arlene said. "He was stingy. Never ran the air conditioning. In the summer, he'd have the front doors open and big fans running."

"And there's the marina," Martinez said. "Dad told us that the business partner, the guy we now know as Cloudy Hair, had an alibi. He was fishing all day and had a receipt from where he put his boat in."

Taleesa chuckled. "That's the flimsiest part of the whole story," she said. "Just because I have a marina receipt, doesn't mean I spent the day fishing. A boat is a vehicle. I could drive it up Red Creek, put it ashore maybe near the highway bridge and walk into town in five minutes. Then walk, or limp, back to the boat when I'm done."

"Speaking of getting downtown," I said, looking at my phone, "It's 9 o'clock right now. We need to stop Jethro before he enters his guilty plea!"

"Call Dad!" Martinez said.

"Cell phones aren't allowed in the courthouse," I said.

"Let's go, kids," Taleesa said. "Atty, you can try to call the court clerk and see if he'll get a message to Dad. Meanwhile, we need to be heading that way. Go, go, go."

We ran to the car, Taleesa kicking up gravel as we sped out of the parking lot. I think it's the first time I ever saw Taleesa put a car in gear without asking us twice if our seat belts are on. Now, suddenly, she was a speed demon. Seventy, eighty, almost ninety miles an hour.

"No answer from the court clerk," I said. "Just a message."

"You have the number for Judge Grover's secretary," she said.

"I'll try it," I said. Nothing. "Gaaaah! No cell phone coverage here! I hate when that happens."

Behind us, a siren.

"Oh, no," Taleesa said. "Getting pulled over. Keep trying to call, Atty."

On the side of the road, we waited for what felt like hours while the deputy, parked behind us, talked on his radio. Why wouldn't he just come up and write us a ticket? Come on!

Finally, he stood beside us. "Driver's license and registration, please," Taleesa handed them over. More agonizing wait. Then: "So, ma'am, what's the hurry?"

"You explain it, Atty," Taleesa told me. "You know the case."

I took a deep breath as I quickly went through the whole case again.

". . . and so we have to get to court and present that evidence as soon as possible."

The deputy stood there poker-faced, his eyes behind dark

glasses. When I was done, he just kept staring, like I hadn't said a thing.

"So, you're Atty Peale, the dog lawyer," he said.

"I'm Atty Peale," I said. "A dog advocate. Can't call myself a lawyer."

"*Colonel* Atticus Peale," he said.

"Not a real colonel of anything," I said, sighing. "It's just an honorary title."

"An appointment from the governor?" he said. "Lieutenant colonel, aide-de-camp to Governor Fischer King."

"That's what it says on the paperwork," I said. "Really, I don't see—"

"Hold on, Colonel," the deputy said. Then he turned to the radio on his shoulder. "Dispatch, Unit 42. I'm going to be out of service for about twenty minutes. I'm escorting a member of the governor's staff to the Strudwick County Courthouse." He handed Taleesa her license. "Just follow me, ma'am, and try to keep up."

And off we went. Faster than I've ever gone before.

"You know," Taleesa said. "It's cool that my daughter's a colonel."

"Damn straight," I replied.

So, I've told you again and again how courtrooms and jails aren't like what you see in the movies. Well, this was kind of like the movies.

We burst into the courtroom in our beach clothes—colorful shorts, flip-flops, T-shirts—so fast that the deputy by the door didn't even have time to stop us. The door swung over and hit the wall with a bang that echoed off the green tile. I had sunglasses on my head and a forbidden cell phone in hand. Martinez, for some reason, was now wearing floaties.

We could see Dad and Jethro at the defendant's table. Jethro was looking handsome in a charcoal gray suit. And he was *standing*.

If you've ever been in a courtroom you know that just about the only time a defendant stands up in the courtroom is to say "Guilty" or "not guilty." Or to hear a jury say the same. We were just in time.

So here's what I didn't expect: at the other table stood a young white man with thick black hair, in a nice-fitting dark suit. This was the prosecutor, the guy who was arguing that Jethro was guilty. *It wasn't Backsley Graddoch.* I had always assumed Graddoch would be on the other side in this case. I don't know why. There are plenty of lawyers in the world. In fact, Graddoch was sitting calmly in the audience, legs crossed lazily, a couple of rows behind where Dad stood.

In the center was Judge Grover, looking like he was ready to snatch every one of us bald. I don't know if I explained this, but making a commotion in a courtroom is, in any judge's eyes, just about the worst thing you can do. Contempt of court. A judge can throw you right into jail for it, without a trial.

We all stood there staring at each other for a second, trying to think what to say. It was so quiet you could hear a floaty squeak. I took a deep breath.

"*If it please the court,*" I said, and I said it loud.

Judge Grover stood up. Judges never stand up. It's the judge equivalent of turning into a megazord.

"IT DOES NOT PLEASE THE COURT, Miss Peale," he said. He turned to Dad. "This court has been very open to this young lady's arguments, but let me tell you, Paul Peale, if this keeps up I'll be holding *you* in contempt."

"Paul," Taleesa said. "Paul, this is an emergency. You've got to stop. You've got to hear us, now, Judge. We have important information, and it's about this case."

Grover plopped down in his chair again. "I'm not sure this case is any of your business, Mrs. Peale," he said. "Mr. Gersham, in consultation with *his attorney*, is here to change his plea to guilty and accept what looks like a pretty generous sentence. Is that still your stance, Mr. Gersham?"

"Jethro," Taleesa said. "Look me in the eye. Are you guilty? Did you shoot anybody?"

Jethro didn't say anything. He just started shaking his head vigorously. First, in our direction. Then he turned to the judge, still shaking his head. A tear rolled out of each eye.

Grover shook his head, too, in exasperation.

"That's it," he said. "In my chambers. All of you. Even you, with the rubber duckies on your arm. We're going to straighten this out."

And it *was* all of us. Me, Taleesa, Martinez, Dad, deputies, the prosecutor: everybody, oddly, except for Jethro, who had to go back to a cell. Even Backsley Graddoch was there, for some reason, in the back of the room. Martinez and I walked Judge Grover through the whole Easy/Edward story. A couple of times. Maybe we're not so good at explaining things we've just discovered.

"And then we headed here, Your Honor," I said in closing. "As quick as we could. I'm truly sorry for barging in, but I couldn't see any other way."

Judge Grover leaned back in his swivel chair and rubbed his face in exasperation.

"Well, I can tell you this," he said. "I will not be accepting a guilty plea today."

He stared Dad in the eye for a few seconds. Then he turned to the prosecutor the same way.

"Like the song says," Grover said. "Everybody's looking like they're supposed to, but ain't nobody looking very good. We've got a man who apparently can't read, but he's signed a typed confession. We've got a potential second suspect who doesn't appear to have been questioned very thoroughly. And on the defense side, we've got a lawyer who's willing to let his client plead even though there may be a bunch of holes in the case. Peale, why couldn't you and Mr. Graddoch find the things these children found?"

Now I was shaking my head. "Wait," I said. "Backsley Graddoch is on Jethro's side?"

"I'm just helping out a bit," Graddoch said. "Not writing anything. Just doing a little research, collecting some information. Just like you were doing a couple of days ago in Jethro's neighborhood, or so his neighbors tell me."

"So you're the lawyer-man the neighbors said they talked to," I said.

"He's doing it pro bono," Dad said. "For free. In his off time."

"But you're the lawyer for Strudwick County," I said.

"In civil cases," he said. "This is a different kind of case.

And unlike some people, I got the court's permission to stick my nose in it."

"I don't get it," Martinez said. "Why would you get involved? And for free?"

Graddoch shrugged. "Same as you," he said. "Jethro's my friend. I hate to see a man I know get strapped to a table and put to death. Not when I can help get him a deal, and maybe an appeal, where he'll see the sun again someday."

Grover held up a sheaf of papers. "I'm not even going to get into what kind of damn fool would sign *this* deal if he knew he were innocent," he said. "What I really want to know is: as smart as all y'all lawyers in this room are, how did you miss these things that a couple of children were able to uncover? Smart people with law degrees. What do these children have that y'all don't?"

"Hope," Taleesa said, still sniffling.

She'd been crying, off and on, ever since Jethro first shook his head at her. She turned around to look at all the faces in the room.

"None of y'all have been *in* the system, have you?" she said. "No. My father was in the system a few times, for little stuff. County jail. Some of the things he went to jail for, he did. Some of them he didn't. After a while, he gave up. After seeing a judge tell him 'guilty' when he wasn't. After saying he was guilty when he wasn't so he could come home to me quicker. At some point he just lost hope. Not hope in himself or hope in me but hope in y'all. Hope that you'd really hear a man when he says he's not guilty. Hope that you'd stop churning people in one door and out the other and maybe stop to give a man a real trial. And once you give up that hope, you don't come through the courthouse doors the same way you used to. You don't hope for justice. You just put on your armor and hold your breath. Maybe you hold your breath for a month. Maybe for years."

Grover pulled a handkerchief out of his coat and handed it to Taleesa.

"Your point is well taken, Mrs. Peale," he said. "We're given too little, by the state and the taxpayer, to do the job we're really supposed to do. If we held a trial in every case that came to us, I couldn't finish this week's docket in a year."

"I don't care," Taleesa said. "I don't care how much work it takes. Jethro doesn't care how much work it takes. None of us do."

There was a long, uncomfortable silence, interrupted only by Taleesa's sniffles. Backsley Graddoch was the first to speak.

"Maybe this is not a good time," he said. "But it occurs to me that I owe Colonel Peale an explanation. I'm sure that to you, I look like a big meanie, always stepping up to fight a little girl in court. I'm a big boy, I can take that. It's my job. If it's ever seemed like I take it too personally, if I've ever seemed angry about you, this is why. I've seen the court shuffle hundreds of young men through the door to jail. Men who don't own a Sunday shirt to wear in court, men who don't know to stand up straight and say 'sir' and 'ma'am' until a judge tells them to. They come in and they go out so fast. And here's a young woman who wants to take up the court's valuable time for animals, when so many human beings come in and out as if pleading guilty to a crime were as common as cashing a check. Maybe I should have said that more plainly from the start. I just want more time for the people who need an advocate."

Dad sighed. "I see what you mean," he said. "And yet, with all our passion for justice, you and I didn't manage to get a real trial for our man—for our friend. Did we?"

"No," Graddoch said. "No, we didn't."

16

"You're a jerk," Reagan Royall said. "You saved a guy from the electric chair and you didn't bring me along! What kind of friend are you?"

"Alabama doesn't have the electric chair," I said." We inject people with poison. And nobody was going to inject him with poison. He was signing a plea deal to avoid exactly that."

Jethro didn't plead guilty, of course. But clearing his name didn't work as fast as I thought it would. After we broke up the plea hearing, they sent him right back to jail. Dad said he'd be out in a few days, released without bail because he's no longer considered a "flight risk." The cops were pretty sure they could let Jethro go home without him running away.

"It's a sign that they know they'll probably drop the charges eventually," Dad said. "Down the road, when it won't sound like such a drastic shift."

The hammer didn't fall on Gary Dudley—Cloudy Hair—just yet, either. They brought him in for questioning, and he had his lawyer present from the start. I'm told he didn't give the investigators anything glaringly obvious. But a bunch of other stuff popped up that fit our theory of the case nicely. Folks at the marina said Dudley returned to the marina without any fish that day, and that he had a limp when he came back that afternoon, and told people he injured himself falling out of his boat, which didn't make a whole lot of sense. Deputies even found a red ball cap under the seat of his boat.

There wasn't any video from the pawnshop itself. But a camera at a service station on the corner caught an image of a dog limping past, leaving a trail of blood. The same camera caught Jethro strolling toward the pawnshop and back, long after Easy went by. The police had watched the video before, but at the time they didn't think the part with the dog was relevant.

I can't tell you how I know those details. They're not from Dad. I have my sources. I'm a colonel, you know.

And word of the whole thing just seemed to get out there. Cloudy Hair was free, but I bet that anywhere he went, he was hearing the same thing I was: that Jethro was innocent, that the cops were looking at Gary Dudley closely, that some meddling kids had solved the case. With their faithful dog. All we needed was a van and Scooby Snacks, I guess.

And Scooby himself. Now that Easy was pretty much cleared of biting without provocation, we had a new reason to look for him: We could bring him home safely to Megg. And deputies were on the lookout, too, now, because Easy was a walking, barking piece of evidence.

It's weird to be congratulated for solving a murder. Particularly in the hallway, while your ex-sort-of-boyfriend is holding another girl's hand.

"Atty, I heard you save a guy from prison," Premsyl said. "Pretty cool. It will look good on a college application."

See? Weird.

"Saved," I said. "The past tense of save is saved."

Premsyl shook his head. "Atty, you're still the same girl I broke up with," he said, brushing a fist playfully past my chin. Braces Girl surveyed me with a lordly look and they turned and walked away.

"Zumpfink bothering you?" Reagan prodded, imitating Premsyl's accent. "Can't keep your feelings in Czech?"

I dismissed Premsyl and girlfriend with a wave of the hand. "Not them necessarily," I said. "But look at this. Look at this hallway closely. What do you see?"

I'll tell you what I saw: boy-girl pairs. Everybody was coupling up, talking beside lockers, walking together in the hallway, flirting anxiously. It was mating season all of a sudden, and somehow I'd missed it.

"The Halloween Dance," Reagan said. "Didn't you see the signs? Everybody's looking for a date. You were too busy saving the world to notice. What, does it bother you?"

"Not exactly," I said. "I think it bothers me that it doesn't bother me. Is there something wrong with me that I don't want to be a part of this?"

"Not at all," Reagan said. "You and I are destined for much better boyfriends than we can get here. Much cooler situations. All these people are pairing up out of fear. Because they think if you can't get a date to the seventh grade dance, you'll die old and alone in a house full of cats. And no one will come to feed the cats for days, and they'll eat your face to stay alive."

"Well, I want to die old," I said. "And I kind of take comfort in the idea that cats would eat my face. I mean, note to self, get a cat-sitter. But if they're really hungry and I'm dead, I hope they *would* eat my face."

"I want cats to eat my face because it's the most goth thing I can think of," Reagan said. "So no dance for you then?"

"On Halloween?" I said. "Heck no. I'm going trick-or-treating with Martinez."

"Oh, isn't that sweet?" Reagan said. "Older sister taking time out to help widdle brother twick or tweet?"

"Help, nothin'!" I said. "I want candy! I love Halloween. I'm going to trick-or-treat for as long as I can. I'm going to trick-or-treat when I'm twenty. I'm going to be a baghead."

I don't know if they have bagheads where you live, but everybody in Houmahatchee knows them. They're the big kids—sixteen, maybe seventeen years old—who come around late at night with a paper sack over their heads to ask if you've got any candy left. Kids who scoff at the idea of trick-or-treating, and say they're too old, but then start feeling remorse as the night goes on and the little kids start bringing home candy. So they reach for the bag and the scissors and make one last pathetic effort to get in on the action.

Of course, there are little bagheads, too. Houmahatchee has lots of kids who are too poor to buy a costume, so they draw a face on a bag. The rule in our house is that little bagheads get to pick through and get all the chocolate and other top treats, while big bagheads get candy corn and peppermints, the yucky stuff.

"Colonel, you are the least punk person I've ever known," Reagan said. "What are you going to be? Little Bo-Peep? Princess Jasmine in a plastic Walmart outfit, like a five-year-old?"

"Oh, come on, this is a high goth holiday," I said. "Surely you haven't given up on trick-or-treat? How old were you when you stopped? What was your last costume?"

Reagan hung her head. "Don't tell anybody, okay? I've never trick-or-treated."

"What?" I said. I couldn't believe it.

"Look, it's a church thing," she said. "They're not super-anti-Halloween at my church, but I guess the thinking is that if it even looks like it's of the devil, a Christian shouldn't be doing it. So they do lock-ins and judgment houses instead. The closest I've ever come to wearing a Halloween costume was when I played a car crash victim in a judgment house."

I'm not a fan of any kind of haunted house. I've never thought it was fun to be chased around in the dark by a guy in an ugly mask with a chainsaw. Judgment houses sound even worse. You go to a church and they walk you through a show where a bunch of rowdy teenagers die in a car crash. The haunty part comes when all the teenagers go to hell because they're not Christians.

"You're coming with us, then," I said to Reagan. "You're going to come and trick-or-treat with us."

"I don't know," Reagan said. "I still think it's kid stuff."

"Come on," I said. "You know you want to."

"I'm not wearing a costume," she said.

"Just linger in the back and pretend you're my big sister," I said. "You're so much taller than me anyway. I'll give you half my candy if you come."

"I'll think about it," she said. "Meanwhile, you need to think about what you're going to be for Halloween."

Just then, I felt a buzz in my pocket. I fished out my cell phone and leaned against my locker to hide it from the teachers.

Do you ever feel those phantom buzzes? You think your phone's ringing when it's not? There was nothing on my phone, not even an annoying message from Princess P. She'd gone completely silent since we cleared Jethro's name, and yet I found myself expecting a message from her, checking my phone every few hours to see what kind of abuse she had for me today.

I scrolled back through the old messages Princess P had sent me.

Princess_P: Pudgy little girl with an annoying voice. You'll die alone.

Princess_P: You should work on saving farm animals. You're such a little piglet.

Princess_P: Oink oink nobody loves me.

Why hadn't I erased these already? Taking occasional glances around to look for teachers, I erased Princess_P's messages one by one. I hadn't responded to a message from her in weeks. I wished there was a way I could show her up, a way to prove I wasn't really bothered by her, without meeting her on her chosen battlefield.

Then I had an idea.

"I've decided," I told Reagan. "I know what I'm going to be for Halloween."

Taleesa is kind of an expert on body acceptance. You know, the whole idea of accepting your body in the size and shape that it is. She's written more than a dozen articles about body acceptance for magazines. Funny, but most of those magazines are the ones that have all the photos of skinny-minnie models in them. Still, Taleesa knows as much about the topic as anybody I know.

"You're the one who decides when you're overweight," Taleesa said. "If you can't run and play the way you'd like to, if you get out of breath before you want to, it's time to lose weight. There are people who'll think you're beautiful no matter how big you get, and there are people who will call you fat no matter how skinny you get. The right weight isn't about looks, it's about being able to do what you want."

I never fully understood that until I tried on my Halloween pig suit.

In my family, we go all out for Halloween. So when I told Taleesa I wanted to be a cute pig, she drove all the way to Panama City for the perfect costume. A bright pink mascot outfit full of stuffing. Pudgy stuffed legs, cute three-fingered cartoon hands at the ends of the sleeves. It zipped up in the back, and climbing into it was kind of like burying your face in a beanbag chair—a beanbag chair that smelled like the sweat of all the people who'd rented the costume before.

As soon as Taleesa zipped me up, I thought about her advice on how to know you need to lose weight. In the pig suit, I was definitely too big. I couldn't put my arms down all the way. I couldn't see my feet. Getting out of the bathroom was hard: there was barely enough room for my pig body to wiggle through the open door.

But man, was I cute! The suit was perfectly cartoony, with a big stuffed pig head with a face hole that allowed me to breathe well and make expressions and roll my eyes at people. (There was a pig nose I could have worn, but I liked having my own face in the pig body.) I stood a long time in the mirror, enjoying the mascotty cuteness of every move I made in this outfit. Dancing the Charleston, doing the Cabbage Patch. Pointing, with my three-fingered fabric hooves, was especially adorable.

"Take *that*, Sexy Barmaid costume!" I shouted, pointing. "Take *that*, Sexy Pirate! Take *that*, Naughty Librarian!"

Take that, Princess P!

Still, I could keep up the act only for a little bit at a time. It was *so* hard to move, and Halloween costumes aren't made for southern Alabama. It was seventy degrees outside on Halloween afternoon in Houmahatchee, and under all the stuffing, I was sweating like . . . well, a pig.

I couldn't even reach my own chest. Taleesa had to pin on the finishing touch: a sign that read "NOT HAM." On the back, another: "PIGS ARE FRIENDS, NOT FOOD." Taleesa laughed when I picked up my cell phone and stuffed it into the pig head next to my face, the only place I could carry it.

"How are you even going to use that with pig hooves?" she asked.

We left Dad behind to deal with the bagheads, and we piled into the car. Or tried to. I couldn't get my seat belt around my big belly without help. Taleesa, decked out as a Spanish countess from an opera, had to make several tries to get her skirts into the driver's seat. Martinez shouldn't have had a problem, but he refused to take off his old-timey sea captain hat even in the car. Reagan, the only person not wearing a costume, had to sit in the back and watch him struggle to sit up straight.

"Just take off your giant hat, there, Cap'n Crunch," she said.

"I'm *not* Cap'n Crunch," he said. "I'm an *admiral*. Get it right. I'm *Admiral* Peale."

"Music!" I shouted, pointing to the radio. For some reason, being dressed as a cuddly thing made me feel the power to be bratty and demanding. "I want 'Monster Mash!'"

Taleesa flipped through the stations. Somebody preaching a sermon. Country music. Football talk. And then: ". . . coming home from our house Christmas Eve. You may say there's no such thing as Santa, but, as for me and Grandpa, we believe."

"No way," Martinez said. "*Christmas* music? On Halloween?"

"They get earlier every year," Taleesa said. "Don't be a hater. Christmas music is great. Christmas is the only time most Americans listen to jazz."

"Oooh, leave it on there," Reagan said. "Maybe they'll play the Charlie Brown stuff."

"Or maybe they'll play *The Song*," Taleesa said, looking

over at me with a devilish look. "If they do, Reagan will have to dance with us."

"Dance, what? I ain't dancing," Reagan said.

"It's a family tradition," I explained. "Every year, we wait to hear the first broadcast of the best, most rockinest Christmas song ever recorded." I paused to see if Reagan could guess it.

"Ummm, 'All I Want For Christmas is You' by Mariah Carey?" Reagan said.

"Yes! See, everybody agrees! And we have this tradition: the first time we hear that song, we stop what we're doing and dance. We could be fleeing our burning house, and we'd still stop and dance," I said.

"I'll stop this car if I hear it," Taleesa said. "And we'll all get out."

Reagan slumped in her seat. "Oh, no. This sounds really cheesy. Change the channel."

"Come on," I said. "You have to do it. Just wait; it won't take long."

We drove over to Marjory Estates, Houmahatchee's one really fancy neighborhood. Well, I guess the historic district where we live looks fancy, but it's just normal people who live there. Marjory Estates is one of those places with big houses and little trees, with a gate at the entrance to the neighborhood. The richest people in town live there, and rich people have the best candy.

It was already dark when we piled out of the car and started moving with the crowd from door to door. The candy-givers didn't quite know what to make of us. Well, they knew what to make of *me*.

"Look, it's Napoleon, and Pat Benatar, and a pig!" said one woman who handed out fistfuls of little chocolate candy bars.

"It's Andrew Jackson, and the lady from *The LEGO Movie*, and a pig!" said a gentle old man with big glasses, who invited us to sort through the candy bowl and take just what we want.

"*LEGO Movie*," Reagan huffed. "Why does everybody think I'm in costume?"

"Oh, Phillip," said Glasses Man's wife, nudging him on the shoulder. "Can't you see this one's not in costume? She's the mom."

I got a good laugh out of that one. For the rest of the way through Marjory Estates, I clung to Reagan's shoulder. "You're so cool, Mom, you look like Pat Benatar, whoever that is," I said.

Reagan wasn't listening. She kept looking over her shoulder. "Something's wrong," she said. "See that ugly brown car back there? With the guy in the hat in it? He's just sitting there, but he hasn't let any trick-or-treaters in or out. Creepy."

"You're just being paranoid, Mom," I said. "Life is not a judgment house."

"Don't be offensive," Reagan said. "You realize that's offensive? And I'm serious, that guy is creepy."

I looked back at the brown car, but couldn't see the guy inside, because just as I looked back, the guy turned on his lights and started his engine. Hm.

"Well, let's catch up with Taleesa and Martinez," I said. "Just in case."

We cleaned out Marjory Estates and soon we were back in the car, trolling for new neighborhoods to plunder. Finally, we stopped on Kilby Street, near the historic district, which was lined with old creaky houses like ours, but even smaller. They always put out good Halloween decorations here, and the street was lined with kids.

"Baghead alert," I said as we emerged onto the sidewalk. "I see one or two big kids out already. They may have picked this neighborhood clean before we got here."

"Hat Guy alert," Reagan whispered to me. "The brown car is here again. I think he's following us."

"I wouldn't worry about it," I said. "Everybody's visiting the same few neighborhoods. You're paranoid, I tell you."

Somebody in the neighborhood was offering a backyard haunted house, which Martinez just *had* to wait in line for.

"But we're missing all the candy," I whined.

"You guys are big enough to go by yourselves," Taleesa said. "I'll stay here with him. But promise me you'll stay together. And promise me you'll only go to the end of the street."

"No problem," I said, and Reagan and I took off.

And then we heard it. A mom, parked on the street and waiting for her kids, had the Christmas station on. It was The Song. *I don't want a lot for Christmas. There is just one thing I need.*

I started shaking my piggy fanny.

"Come on, Reagan!" I said. "You gotta dance!" I whipped out all the pig-suit dancing moves I'd tried in the bathroom. I'm pretty sure I saw people from school driving by. I thought I even saw Premsyl, riding in the back seat of the Braxtons' car, with Braces Girl, on their way to the Halloween Dance. I shot my hoof in the air and shouted. Pig suits and Mariah Carey make everything better.

Reagan stood there with her arms crossed. I was just getting going when the mom with the radio drove away.

"Man, Reagan," I said. "For an outlaw, you're no fun. Can't you dance and be crazy?"

I tried to get Reagan to pretend to be my mom at a couple of houses, but I guess the folks there knew me already: they called me Colonel. We were on the way to our third house when I heard a deafening blast of music in my ear.

"Ugh," I said. "I should have turned the ringer off before I stuck my phone in this pig hat." I fished out the phone and handed it to Reagan. "Can you turn it on? I can't do it with pig hands."

Reagan pressed the screen and handed the phone back to me.

"Hello, are you the girl who's looking for the lost dog?" said a man's voice on the other end. "The one with the signs everywhere?"

"That's me," I said.

"Well, I saw him just now, like a minute or two ago, on Kilby Street," the man said.

My heart leaped. We could get Easy back!

"I'm on Kilby right now," I said. "Where did you see him? Where are you?"

"Oh, I drove on by five minutes ago," the man said. "But he was down at the end of the street. Over in the woods near the Ridley house at the dead end."

I looked down the street, then down the street the other

way. Kilby dead-ended into a darkened old abandoned two-story house. On either side, tufts of forest.

"I bet if you hurry, you could still find him there," the man said. I thanked him and hung up.

"Reagan, I've got a caller who says Easy is right over there in the woods next to that house. Let's go!"

I ran as fast as I could, spilling candy behind me. I tumbled over and fell on my piggy knees, then got up and ran faster, leaving my candy bag behind. I was out of breath by the time we got to the dead end.

"EASY!" I shouted. "EDWARD! Come here, boy!"

I hadn't given up on my dog. Now that he was cleared of unprovoked biting, he could be adopted out to some family and live the rest of his life in peace—if we could just find him.

"Reagan, I'll look in the woods on this side, you search that side," I said.

"We're not supposed to split up," Reagan said.

"It's an emergency," I said. "Just do it. Go on!"

I plunged into the woods on my side, shouting for Easy. I had planned to turn on the flashlight on my phone, but my piggy hands wouldn't let me. I just pressed ahead, batting aside branches and shouting for my dog.

And then I stopped to listen for him.

I could hear Reagan on the other side of the house, calling Easy's name. Very distantly, I could hear the sound of organ music from the haunted house down the street.

And then I heard something moving in the leaves. I knew from the start that it wasn't Easy. It was a person. You could tell they were human footsteps. Crunch, crunch crunch.

That was when I realized what I'd done. I was *that* girl, the one who stupidly wandered off alone into the dark on Halloween, where some strange man lay in wait. Those stories, the ones you read in the newspaper, are true. And I was about to become one of them.

I was pretty deep in the woods. It was so dark, all I could see was the outlines of leaves on the trees silhouetted against the dim orange glow from the streetlights. But I could see the outline of the man as he stepped forward. A man in a ball cap, just like Reagan had said. And when he took off his ball cap to wipe his brow, I could see a halo of white hair outlined in that light.

Cloudy Hair! I took a couple of steps backward, hoping to blend into the trees and hide myself, I guess. Though it was so dark, I had no idea what kind of dark I was stepping out of and what kind of dark I was stepping into. I must have made a rustling noise, because I could see Gary Dudley's head suddenly turn my way.

Have you ever felt real fear? I mean, a kind that turns you inside out, in an instant? I felt as though someone had poured some kind of hot acid into my body. I felt sick but unable to barf. I felt capable of running a thousand miles but somehow unable to take a step.

In an instant, Cloudy Hair was on me. His arm around my neck, one of his feet trying to sweep my feet out from under me.

"You little piggy, let's see how you squeal when I slit your throat!" he said.

It was then that I caught a dull flash of light. In his free hand, Cloudy Hair had a knife.

I really don't know how I got free of him. The pig suit was so thick, it was hard for me to tell when he had hold of me and when he didn't. But I did get free, rolled to the right for a few turns to get fully clear of Cloudy Hair, then sprang up and ran. I bet I've never run like that before in my life: full tilt into complete darkness, tripping over roots and popping back up again, slamming into branches and going right on like a machine. In my mind, Cloudy Hair was just inches behind me, and there was no time to stop and check if I was right.

Finally I ran out of the woods and into some light. The back of some kind of store. There was one dim streetlight, a pair of dumpsters, and a little alleyway between the back of the store and a cinder-block wall. I took off at a sprint down the alley, thinking I could run around to the front of the store and be among people again.

Wrong.

Passing the dumpsters, I came to a dead end. More wall, cinder block on all three sides. Just as I realized my predicament, I tripped and tumbled.

Cloudy Hair was there, at the entrance to the alley. With a gun. And wild, wide eyes.

"Go ahead and scream, piggy," he said. "It's Halloween. Nobody will take you seriously."

Okay, lawyer, I thought. *Talk your way out of this one. What do you say?*

"Don't shoot me," I said, simply. "Please don't shoot me."

And then all the fear inside me broke. I started weeping. Snotty, sloppy crying. Thoughts flashed through my mind. Dad handing me McNutters for the first time, Martinez in the car with his video game, Taleesa helping me put on my pig suit. All of that, all those memories, would vanish forever if he pulled the trigger. Death, and the permanence of it, is a hard thing to take in all at once.

"Please, mister," I said. "Don't kill me."

"Well, now I have to, don't I?" Cloudy Hair said. "Not only are you testifying against me in one murder, but now you can testify that I did this, too. Sorry, you've gotta go."

"Anything," I said. "I'll do anything."

"Really?" Cloudy Hair replied, still pointing the gun at me. "What if I ask you to take it all back? Tell the grand jury you don't really think I did it. Can you do that?"

I nodded. I'm sorry, readers, but that's what I did. A man pulled a gun on me and I promised to take back the most important thing I've ever said.

"Promise me you'll testify against Jethro? Say that he put you up to accusing me? Say that you were afraid of him?"

I nodded, still weeping, on my hands and knees. "Say it!" Cloudy Hair shouted.

"I promise," I said.

Cloudy Hair smirked.

"It's good to hear you say it," he said. "I'm gonna kill you anyway. I just wanted to see how easy it was to make you say it. You're so weak. A pudgy, soft freak. 'Oink oink, nobody loves me!'"

Suddenly something fell into place. Something so shocking, it overwhelmed my fear for a minute.

"Wait a minute," I said. "You're Princess P! You've been texting me all this time!"

Cloudy Hair nodded. "You see, you can't get away. I'm

inside your head. I'm there all the time. You can't get away from me. I win."

All the texts from Princess P flooded back. It did, in a weird way, make sense. Cloudy Hair knew, when nobody else knew, that Easy was evidence in a crime. He knew that every time we posted a flyer with Easy's photo, every time someone forwarded the news story about him, there was a chance someone would recognize the murder victim's dog and start asking questions. So all of that trolling—the fat pig stuff, the stuff about my mom's suicide—it was all just a dumb, weak attempt to make my work harder for me.

Suddenly, I was angrier than I was scared. I stood up on my little piggy feet, pointed a hoof right in Cloudy Hair's face.

"Just hold it right there," I said. "All this time you've been lecturing me about who's a freak who can't survive. But you *killed your own brother-in-law*. For money!"

Cloudy Hair just stared at me with dead eyes, but he didn't shoot. I took another step forward.

"You couldn't cut it in business, so you killed your best friend!" I said. "You couldn't cover that up, so you're going to kill a twelve-year-old girl!"

Cloudy Hair didn't move. I took another step.

"I may be a pig, I may be weak, but you're a MUR-DERER!" I shouted.

What happened next happened very fast. I could see Cloudy Hair blink, dumbfounded, and I knew I'd landed an insult that really hurt him. I could see the muscles in his forearm flex as he started to pull on the trigger. I heard nothing, but I did see a flash, just a blip of light on the end of his gun. And I saw a blur of black and white that seemed to pull Cloudy Hair down to the ground.

It was Easy! Where he came from or how he happened on us, I don't know, but in an instant, Easy had Cloudy Hair on the ground, his teeth locked into the old man's upper thigh.

I don't know if you have ever seen a man attacked by a dog, but it isn't a pretty sight. Cloudy Hair screamed like he was being eaten alive, and Easy wasn't letting up. There was blood. I saw Cloudy Hair's gun on the ground, and initially thought of picking it up and holding him at gunpoint. But not with pig hands. So I kicked it, and it skittered into the leaves.

Later, as he struggled to crawl across the alleyway, Dudley dropped his knife, too. I kicked it away.

Then I heard a blip from a police car's siren. At the exit of the alleyway, cops were silhouetted in red-and-blue light.

"Don't hurt the dog!" I shouted, throwing myself on top of Easy. "The dog is fine! The dog's protecting me! Don't shoot!"

Dudley tried to limp away, and got caught and cuffed by one cop. The other came up to me and Easy, hands held open. It was Troy Butler.

"Atty Peale?" he said. "Is that you in there? Are you injured?"

Butler's voice was shaking a little, something I'd never heard from him. That scared me. Was I injured? I started patting myself down with my piggy hands, looking for a bullet hole.

"Looks like you had a close call," Troy said, reaching up to touch the side of my head. I heard a POP of breaking string and Troy held out a fuzzy costume pig ear. "You're lucky, Not Ham. He shot your ear half off. An inch or two down and to the right, and that bullet would have hit your head, instead of your costume."

From time to time, people ask me if working at an animal shelter is fun.

"Yes," I tell them. "But I don't think my shelter experience is typical."

Not every shelter volunteer gets to meet the governor. And even though that's not anything any sensible kid really wants to do, meeting the governor might turn out to be useful after all.

And not every shelter volunteer gets a free pig suit. The costume company wouldn't take the suit back, with an ear blown off and stains on it from crawling around in the woods. They wouldn't even cut us some slack because I was the victim of attempted murder. (I know they knew about it. It was all over the news as far away as Orlando.) Dad and Taleesa had to fork over $300 for it, and because we didn't know how to clean the thing, it's hanging in my closet now, dirty and smelly as it was the night of the attack.

Toni says that's probably not healthy. Toni's my therapist. Yes, I have a therapist now. I'm talking about a therapist for your head—a psychologist—not a therapist for your body. Dad and Taleesa set up weekly sessions for me because of Cloudy Hair's attack on me.

Being a crime victim is weird, even if you're the lucky one the bullet missed. After they hauled Gary Dudley away that night, a couple of young deputies—Sam and Lizzie were their names—examined me like I was a captured alien. Or really, I guess, they examined the pig suit while I was still in it, taking photos and collecting fuzz samples in little bags. Then the paramedics did a medical check on me. Then we went back to the jail, which is also the sheriff's office headquarters, and they made me tell the story of the attack again and again, which I told the same way again and again just like I told it to you. Even the part where, with a gun pointed at me, I renounced everything I believe in. That part seemed to bother me more than it bothered anybody else.

Still, the whole story bothered somebody, because they gave Dad and Taleesa a bunch of brochures about post-traumatic stress disorder and warned them that I should get into therapy to avoid any problems down the road, including— duh duh *duuuh*—depression. Dad had me set up with Toni the next day.

I like therapy, because I like Toni. She's in her late twenties, I guess, and has a cute short haircut—like, boy-short—and big, thick, but totally fashionable glasses, and she's always wearing cool retro fashions, like combat boots and flannel shirts. Her office shelves are full of plaques with punchy slogans: "Well-behaved women rarely make history," or "Be the change you want to see in the world." She even has a cross-stich sampler that says "Hell is other people."

"That looks familiar," I said the first time I saw it. "Where did you get it?"

"I bought it from a middle-school kid on Etsy," she said.

Toni wants me to talk about Cloudy Hair, about my bouts of what she calls "depression," about my mom and how she died. But I try my best to talk instead about Toni's love life. I know she has kids—I've seen the photos on her desk—but there's no wedding ring. And her desk also has photos of her hiking and canoeing with cute hipster guys. I really want to know the story there.

"I imagine you living this perfect life," I say. "Climbing mountains, growing huge vegetables in your garden, flitting from boyfriend to boyfriend, writing papers about all of us screwed-up people in Alabama and presenting them at a conference in Stockholm."

"That's transference," Toni said. "There's a point in therapy when the therapist becomes your idol. It will pass. Usually we've made more progress than this before transference happens."

Toni hasn't said it, but I'm pretty sure she thinks I'm tough patient to crack. I have a problem with this whole post-traumatic stress disorder thing. I mean, if I get shot at, and later I have nightmares or flashbacks about it, how is that a *disorder*? I mean, isn't that normal for a person who's been shot at?

Anyway, Toni says I need to work out some issues in case I have to testify against Gary Dudley in court. But you and I know that won't happen. If Jethro Gersham felt like he had to cut a plea deal—when he knew all along he was innocent—then surely Cloudy Hair will cut a deal, too. After all, they've got a statement from the victim, a weapon with his prints on it, and a thousand photos of a pig costume with a bullet hole in it. And that's just from his attempt to murder me, not to mention the murder he successfully committed.

Jethro is of course out of prison, and maybe that's what I really need therapy for. What do you say to a guy who's been through this? He came by the house a few days ago, to say thank you. He brought me flowers and brought Martinez a football.

"I thank God for you," he said to me. "I know the light of God is in you, because you saved me. You saved my life."

For once, I kept my mouth shut. I could have said that Martinez did most of the work on his case, which was true, and I could have said that his life wasn't really at stake because he was already about to plead down to a non-capital charge. Instead, I just hugged Jethro, and that seemed like exactly the right thing.

Taleesa says flowers are losing their smell. It's something about the way they grow them, in greenhouses. Sniff the flowers on sale at the grocery store and you'll see. But the flowers I got from Jethro that day—purple, spiky-looking blooms, sprigs of green ferny stuff—had a perfumey smell to them. I still wonder where he got them.

We didn't really see much of Jethro after that visit, which I guess was just as well. The last time we drove by his place, the city's warning sign was gone, the yard was trimmed nicely, and the painting was done. I like to think of him puttering around the house happily all day like McNutters, though even McNutters has times when the hot tub won't heat and the cork won't come out of the champagne bottle.

According to Wikipedia, kids suffering from post-traumatic stress sometimes experience regression. In other words, after a big shock, you might go back, for comfort's sake, and start doing little-kid things you did a couple of grades ago. I tried to milk that for all it was worth, reserving plenty of time to play with McNutters in his dollhouse.

It was fun at first, but after a while I started to think that McNutters's life of luxury wasn't as interesting as it used to be. Why lounge in the hot tub when you can climb mountains and fight injustice, the way I imagined Toni did in her off hours?

Maybe this "transference" was really a thing. I found myself thinking more and more about Toni's life during my daily work at the shelter. Cleaning litter boxes, walking dogs, devouring name-your-baby books and thesauruses in search of new names and descriptions to liven up the pet-of-the-week column. It all felt like a long climb up a mountain, but I wasn't always sure we were getting any higher.

"Megg," I said one day. "Remind me again why we can't have a no-kill shelter like they have in San Francisco or wherever? A shelter that commits to not killing a single animal?"

"I don't think those no-kill shelters are always as no-kill as they make out to be," Megg replied. "I think some of them are just less-kill shelters. And state law pretty much says we have to kill the dogs that bite. But I never said we *can't* have a no-kill shelter. There are just a lot of reasons *we don't*. A lot of people here can barely afford to feed themselves, much less their pets."

"Maybe we can find a way to be the first poor county to have a no-kill shelter. An honest-to-gosh place where no animal has to be killed," I said. "Maybe there's a way no one's considered."

"Maybe it's possible," Megg said. "But it would take a while. It might take twenty years."

"I guess we should start planning now, then," I said.

Megg smiled at me. "Atty, I think you could do just about anything you set your mind to," she said. "Bring me a twenty-year plan to set up a no-kill shelter and I'll present it to the county commission. I'll put everything I have behind it, I promise."

And so here I am, on my bed with my dog, about to start writing my plan.

Oh, I didn't tell you about Easy? He's ours now. After the incident with Cloudy Hair, Taleesa gave in and said we could adopt him if J. D. Ambrose's family didn't claim him. Megg took the dog to Ambrose's only heir, the same sister who was married to Cloudy Hair, and was told she and the dog could both go rot.

So now Easy sleeps at the foot of my bed. And when I go to school, he sleeps on the wood floor in the foyer. And when I come back, he sleeps in front of the couch at my feet. He's like a real-life McNutters, living a life of luxury.

And he's a great help if you're writing. I've started talking out loud when I write, bouncing ideas off him. He listens earnestly to everything but never says a word, good or bad.

Like just now, when I'm telling you and Easy this story, when I should be writing the introduction to my twenty-year plan.

"What should I start with?" I say, looking down at Easy. "I need an inspiring story of an animal someone saved from being put down."

Easy yawns.

"What's that, boy?" I say. "That's a great idea. I'll start with you."